FINDING HER
PERFECT FAMILY

Fleeing as far as she can from an unhappy home life, Amelia Knight arrives at the tropical island of Trinita to work as a nanny at the Grenville estate. As she battles insects and tropical heat, she must also fight her increasing attraction to baby Lucio's widowed father, Leo Grenville — a man whose heart has been broken, and thus is determined never to love again. Amelia must conquer stormy weather and reveal a desperate secret before she can find her perfect family to love forever.

Books by Carol MacLean
in the Linford Romance Library:

WILD FOR LOVE
RESCUE MY HEART
RETURN TO BARRADALE
THE JUBILEE LETTER
FROZEN HEART
JUNGLE FEVER
TO LOVE AGAIN
A TEMPORARY AFFAIR

CAROL MacLEAN

FINDING HER PERFECT FAMILY

Complete and Unabridged

LINFORD
Leicester

First published in Great Britain in 2016

First Linford Edition
published 2016

A catalogue record for this book is available
from the British Library.

ISBN 978–1–4448–2876–4

Published by
F. A. Thorpe (Publishing)
Anstey, Leicestershire

Set by Words & Graphics Ltd.
Anstey, Leicestershire
Printed and bound in Great Britain by
T. J. International Ltd., Padstow, Cornwall

This book is printed on acid-free paper

1

The beast watched Amelia speculatively. It was at least the length of a man, with mean, beady yellow eyes. An alarming row of teeth lined its long snout. It lay lazily across the path, not in any hurry to move out of Amelia's way.

'Shooo!' *Yeah, great Amelia. That really worked.* What was the thing, anyway? Science had never been her strong point. It looked like a crocodile or an alligator. And did it really matter what it was, except that it was big and scary and blocking her way? She gripped her pull-along suitcase more tightly and looked longingly ahead. The path sliced through the sweating jungle and led, as far as she knew, to the front gates of the Grenville estate. If the taxi driver hadn't dropped her off so fast and sped off, she might actually be confident of that fact.

She could almost hear her father's voice: *You did what? You left the airport without a map of where you were going? It's typical of you, Amelia. You really haven't a clue. I'll sort it out for you.* The slight sneer. The patronising tone. Amelia's chin trembled and she took a deep breath, pushed her shoulders back, and stood up straight to her maximum five-foot-three. William, her father, wasn't here, but she was, and she could handle this.

The jungle was a cacophony of chirps and bellows and buzzing around her, and the air was hot and moist like someone had wrapped a damp flannel over her skin. Tiny bees hovered unpleasantly close to her. It was a far cry from the city of London, and it was time to move.

Her heart thudding in her chest, Amelia stepped away from the comforting solidity of the man-made path onto the squelch of the rainforest floor.

Within minutes the jungle had swallowed her up. It was dark under the canopy and, high above, the fronds quivered as monkeys leapt from tree to tree, calling and hooting.

I will not cry, she told herself sternly. Her new pick-me-up sandals sank into soft leaf litter with every step and were already mud-streaked. She was sweating horribly in her new silk blouse, and she'd ripped her skirt on a hooked branch. Tears welled up and she scrubbed them away furiously. *I can do this. All I have to do is walk parallel to the path. Even a loser like me can manage that.* It was like walking in treacle, it was so clumsy and slow.

The canopy thinned abruptly and she half-ran into a vast open clearing, pulling her suitcase clunkily. A man was chopping at the foliage with a dangerous-looking machete. His bronzed arm muscles rippled with the effort, and Amelia felt her stomach twist. He was darkness like a panther, with a thick head of black hair and dark golden eyes, which he turned on her. Equally black brows drew together in surprise at her sudden appearance at the edge of the jungle. His scruffy jeans and ragged shirt suggested he was one of the Grenville's estate workers. Perhaps he could escort her to her new employer.

'Hello, I'm looking for the way to Grenville House. Am I on the right track?'

The man stared at her with his unsettling amber eyes; then his lips twitched as if he was amused. 'You don't seem to be on any track,' he said. His voice was deep velvet and seasoned with a hint of an island accent, and for some reason it gave her a little shiver up her spine.

'I was on the path to Grenville, but there was this . . . this thing in the way, so I had to take a diversion,' Amelia said, trying for dignity and failing. She felt a flare of annoyance. Who was he, anyway? She didn't have to explain herself to him. There was something

4

about him, though. The panther image stuck in her mind. He exuded a silent power. Or maybe she was suffering from the effects of heat exhaustion. She plucked at the front of her blouse, trying to waft in some cooler air. He watched her and she blushed, dropping her hand to the safe anchor of the grip of her suitcase.

'A thing?' he asked, and again there was a hint of laughter in his tone. He was mocking her gently, like a big cat playing with its prey.

'I don't know what it was,' she said, wiping away beads of moisture from her forehead. 'A crocodile?'

'Most likely a small caiman,' he said, swinging the machete against the nearest tree as if he had finished with her.

Amelia waited. He swung the blade once more and she heard him mutter something under his breath. He turned back politely to her. 'You want me to take you to the house?'

'Yes, please,' Amelia said gratefully,

ready to wail in relief. She couldn't help flicking a glance at him. He was gorgeous. He couldn't be past his mid-thirties, and he was all lean muscle and angled planes. And tall. He towered over her. But then, most people were taller than her. She'd spent a lifetime looking up. But she'd have to stretch pretty far to kiss him. *As if.*

She was suddenly aware of her bedraggled appearance. Her pale hair had come loose from its smart chignon and curled, limp with the humidity, around her face. She was fairly sure there was a smear of mud on her cheek, and when she checked her toes sticking out from the sandals, they were peat-brown.

'Come along then.' There was a hint of impatience in his voice. She was being a bother to him. Her father had been the master of telling her what a bother she was. Never in so many words, but rather with an expert, exasperated sigh. She should be used to it, but she was disappointed to come on such a long journey only to find she was still a hindrance.

'Do you work for Mr Grenville?' she asked, determined to keep him sweet, at least until he delivered her safely to the door of the house.

'You could say that,' he answered. He swung the machete in powerful blows that split the greenery, and she saw the path emerge in front of them. He lifted her suitcase easily onto one broad shoulder and led the way out of the cloying jungle and on to civilisation without glancing back at her to see if she was following.

'I've got a job up at the house,' she called conversationally, pushing away a snagged vine before it slapped her in the face.

He nodded disinterestedly and strode on. Amelia ran to keep up with him, turning her ankle painfully as one sandal heel caught on a stone. He frowned down at her. 'You could break your ankle in those. Why would you wear such flimsy, impractical shoes here?'

He seemed genuinely to want to know. She opened her mouth and shut it again. She could hardly explain that she'd bought them to give her courage. They were the first bright, colourful items she'd seen as she took her initial walk of freedom along the city's high street. She'd gone straight in and bought them, delighting that there was no one there to tell her they weren't her style and that she should choose again.

She looked at them doubtfully. There was little of the original colour showing now. The leather was bashed and scored from the journey. They looked forlorn. She felt a swift empathy for her sandals. They were out of place and lost here. 'They made me feel good,' she answered honestly. Past tense.

He shook his head and quirked an eyebrow. 'You'll need flat shoes working as a maid.'

'Oh, no — you've got it wrong,' she said, but he strode on and she was talking to his back.

She saw a large white colonial

mansion looming into view, proud and majestic behind wrought-iron gates and high perimeter walls. They were nearly at the house. In a few minutes he would be gone back to the jungle and she would be where she was meant to be. She was strangely reluctant to see him go.

'Do you know Mr Grenville? What's he like to work for?' Amelia asked as the man halted.

'You won't see much of him,' he said abruptly. 'The housekeeper, Mrs Sorrento, sees to everything. As the new maid, you'll take your orders from her.'

'What's he like?' Amelia persisted. He was quite the mystery employer. Her correspondence, and the job interview in response to the advert, had been carried out in London by an agency. All she knew was that he was a single father who needed a carer for his only child.

'He likes his peace and quiet. He wants only to be left alone.'

She shivered despite the heat and gazed up at the mansion. Its windows were blank and opaque, giving nothing away. Had she made a terrible mistake coming here? She had run away blindly from what waited at home — but what had she run to? She had deliberately chosen the furthest-away job from London as possible, forgetting that she'd be all alone. If she needed help, there was no one to turn to.

But that's the point. It's the new, independent me. I can cope with anything that's thrown at me. I have to. What was the alternative? To run back to William? She never could bring herself to call him Father or Dad. Nor did he want her to. So, William it was. He'd love it if she went back to him. He'd ordered her not to go. And when that hadn't worked . . . She didn't want to think about it again. She pushed it down into a dark place inside her and lidded it. No, she was here on Trinita Island, off the coast of South America, and she would see it through.

She turned to politely thank her companion, thinking to ask his name, and screamed. A massive bug on burring wings flew straight at her. It landed on her chest above the open collar of her blouse. She was terrified. It was horrid and shiny. It would bite her for sure.

'Get it off! Please get it off,' she said frantically. No way was she going to touch it. But it had to go, and now!

'Relax. Don't move,' he said calmly. 'It's only a blue click beetle.'

'Only? I don't care what it is. Just remove the damn thing.'

He smiled crookedly, showing even, white teeth; and a sexy dimple appeared in one cheek. Even in her terror, Amelia felt a surge of pure desire for his dark good looks.

'Okay, here we go. Don't be frightened,' he said.

For a moment she wasn't sure who he was talking to, her or the ugly bug. Then she felt the touch of his fingers on her bare flesh and a spark ignited in her blood, heating her from the inside. His eyes widened as if in shock and his touch lingered. Then the beetle was gone, flown from his hand, and Amelia was left with a burning brand on her chest.

Incredibly, he leaned in once more to touch her lightly where the beetle had landed. She thought she would faint. If only he would trail his fingers further south, dipping down below the line of her collar, stroking and teasing her flesh. She gave an inaudible moan. His finger stopped and withdrew.

'You have a small abrasion from the creature's legs. It didn't mean you any harm, but it does have hooks that can scratch. When you get inside, ask Mora for some antiseptic.'

The shutters were down again, his manner stiff and formal. But Amelia would have sworn that he'd felt it too — an electricity that had sparked between them when they touched. She could no longer deny that she found him dangerously attractive. It didn't mean she had to act on it. It was animal, feral, like a panther itself. She didn't need that. She was here to concentrate on her fresh start and new employment. Still, the memory of his fingers tracing her skin sent a thrill coursing through her that she couldn't suppress.

'Are there lots of those bugs about?' she asked in distaste.

'You'll be quite safe from them in the house. Mora won't stand for the wildlife in her domain. Once you start working you'll be too busy to notice them; the maids are kept very busy, I'm afraid. It's a large house, and the tropics can be unkind to bricks and mortar.'

His tone was dismissive of her. Clearly he didn't admire her reaction to the 'wildlife'. Amelia tried not to care what he thought of her. A sneaking suspicion flickered in her head. He was awfully familiar with the household and someone called Mora. Could Mora be the housekeeper, Mrs Sorrento, he'd referred to? Was it likely that he was just an estate worker, despite his shabby clothes?

He leant against a palm tree, watching her: a man relaxed and confident on his own property.

'I'm not here to be the new maid,' Amelia admitted. She wriggled her dirty toes at the confession. He raised his eyebrows in a silent question, so she went on. 'I'm the new nanny.'

He shot upright and stared at her. Amelia stared back up at him, causing an ache in her neck. His expression was thunderous.

'You, a mere wisp of a girl? What was Mora thinking of? How old are you?'

She quailed beneath his black scowl. What was wrong? She tilted her chin up defiantly. 'I'm older than I look. I'm twenty-seven. I know I'm petite, but I'm strong and fit and quite capable of doing the work.'

'Doing the work? You make it sound like an office job. This is my son we're talking about. What experience could you possibly have that's enough for this task?'

So he was Leo Grenville, the father of

Lucio Grenville, the baby boy who needed a nanny to replace the last one who'd gone at very short notice. Had the nanny left of her own accord, or had Leo Grenville sacked her? He was still smouldering with anger, waiting for her to answer.

'I've nannied for the past five years, so I have plenty of experience. Who were you expecting?'

He paced up and down, his jaw tight. His tawny eyes flashed. 'A much older woman. Someone with maturity who can protect my son.'

'I'm more than capable of protecting him,' Amelia argued. Protecting the child from what? The house was already shielded and prison-like behind the perimeter stone walls and the locked gates. She'd noted the code box and entry system. There was a lot of security here. It was more than adequate to look after a six-month-old baby.

'Capable, you?' he drawled. 'Have you seen yourself? Your clothes are torn, your shoes are a mess, and your hair . . . ' He tugged a curl to demonstrate its state, his palm brushing momentarily against her cheekbone. An ember sparked in her skin. She wanted more, even in his anger. But he stood back as if burnt by their contact.

'You were lost in the forest within minutes of your arrival. You can't even cope with a small click beetle.' He shrugged in frustrated disbelief.

Small? She'd hate to see a full-size beetle. 'I can cope. I got a shock, that's all. This is my first visit to South America and to Trinita. But I adapt fast.'

She hoped it was true, because she was fighting for her job now and it hadn't even begun. She couldn't lose it on the first day. She had bought a one-way ticket and didn't have enough money to buy one back to England. And even if she did, there was nothing there for her. William would be only too happy to take her back, under his conditions. Fear of that particular scenario gave her courage and she steeled herself, wishing her heels were higher to give her more authority.

'I can assure you that Lucio will be safe with me.'

His shoulders slumped as his fury left him. 'I'm sorry, but you won't get the chance to prove that. I apologise for my rudeness. I'm not angry at you, but I'm furious at myself. I should never have let this happen. I should have looked at the résumés myself and carried out the interviews personally.' The trace of island in his accent was more pronounced in his emotion. 'I apologise again. You're welcome, of course, to stay the night with us at Grenville House. You must be weary, and I'm sure you could do with freshening up. You can eat a meal with us, and tomorrow I'll personally drive you to the airport.'

His voice was quiet but firm, velvet sheathed around steel. He left her standing there and headed for the house, taking her battered suitcase with him.

Amelia was stunned. She had got the job and lost it, and all without even meeting the little baby, Lucio. It was completely unfair. The old Amelia would have meekly done what she was told. But the newly emerged Amelia wanted something different, something more. If Leo Grenville imagined she was going without a fight, he had another think coming.

2

Amelia sat upstairs on the edge of an enormous king-size bed. The room itself was large but plainly decorated: white walls, dark hardwood furniture, white coverlet. A window was open, and through the mosquito mesh covering it she could feel the pulse of the tropical night. The air was hot and thick and there was a constant chirping of cicadas, a sound so alien and exotic she wanted to cry. It was far distant from the London townhouse where the hum of city centre traffic had kept her company — which was sort of the whole point, she reminded herself.

A great wave of homesickness threatened to overwhelm her. She clenched her fists and pushed her emotions down. This wouldn't do. She had walked out of her life to find something new. Something *better*. She had to find the strength now to make a real go of it. She couldn't scurry back to William and the security of that gilded prison. *She wouldn't.*

She had to convince the man downstairs, Leo Grenville, to let her stay. A little shiver played over her skin when she thought of his sudden displeasure. A mere wisp of a girl — ? He had mocked her assurance that she was capable of looking after his son. She felt again his brief touch against her cheek and the heat ignited by his skin against hers. *Enough, Amelia. It's the tropical heat talking, that's all.*

She kicked off her ruined sandals and decided that a cool shower would help. Perhaps then, when her feet returned to their normal colour and she was well-dressed, she would find the courage to challenge the master of Grenville.

Mora Sorrento had thoughtfully provided small packages of soap and bottles of shower gel along with a bundle of soft, fluffy towels. She had winked at Amelia and smiled as they heard Leo's voice growling from downstairs.

'His bark's worse than his bite,' she said to Amelia, the words lilting gently in her Spanish accent. 'He'll come round to you, you'll see. Please, take your time and freshen up. Dinner will be at eight.'

Now Amelia opened her suitcase and searched through the neat folds of material for something suitable to wear. She'd had to leave so many gorgeous outfits in London when she left so suddenly. She settled on a green silk dress cinched at the waist with a wide belt. The belt buckle pulled in two extra notches and the dress hung a little loosely on her. She'd lost too much weight recently without trying. In the mirror two anxious grey eyes stared back at her.

She swept her fair hair up in an improvised chignon that only emphasised the gauntness of her cheekbones further. With a sigh, she let her hair fall freely around her face instead. It would have to do. She was ready for dinner; there could be no further delays or prevarication. Her heart thumping a little louder than usual, she descended the wide staircase in search of Leo Grenville.

She followed the sound of low voices and found the dining room. Its enormous table was set with two places, and at the far end stood Leo. Before her nerve could fail her, Amelia walked confidently towards him, her hand outstretched in greeting.

'We weren't properly introduced in the jungle. I'm Amelia Knight.' *The new nanny*, she longed to add, but didn't quite dare. She didn't want to see him glower darkly at her again. Instead, she'd love to see the dimple reappear in his right cheek.

'Leo,' he said simply, acknowledging her with a nod of his dark head. He clasped her hand firmly. Little crackles of electricity shot along her arm. Amelia pulled her hand back. Had he noticed?

Had he felt it too?

But he had turned away abruptly to speak to Mrs Sorrento. Amelia sank into her seat. Her heart was pounding. She concentrated on slowing her breathing. Okay, she found her new potential boss devastatingly attractive. She had to stamp it out, now! She needed this job; she was desperate. She wanted to be Lucio's nanny — which was why she had to fight against his father's unnerving animal magnetism and concentrate on persuading him to give her the position.

She looked up to see Leo staring at her quizzically, one brow raised. He was amused at her. Yes, the dimple was back. Did he have to look so gorgeous without trying? He had changed for dinner into a white shirt and khaki bush trousers. The shirt emphasised his tanned skin. She thought again of a panther — relaxed and playful, but dangerous nonetheless. There was a coiled watchfulness about him.

He broke into her fevered thoughts.

'Why are you here, Amelia?'

'I told you. I've come to be a nanny for Lucio.'

He shook his head impatiently. 'Why here particularly, I mean. Trinita is a long way from anywhere. Surely you could find a nanny position in England?'

She'd have trouble finding one in England; William had made sure of that. 'I needed a change of scene,' she told him. It was a partial truth. It would have to do.

'The tropics can be harsh to live in if you're not used to them,' Leo continued, suddenly cold. 'The sun can be unkind to pale complexions.' His eyes flicked over her blonde hair and back to her face.

Amelia flushed angrily. 'Well if you get your way, I won't have a chance to find that out, will I?'

Unexpectedly, Leo threw back his head and laughed. She saw the strong column of his neck and lowered her gaze. 'You don't give up easily. I admire

that. But you can't stay. Lucio needs
. . . a lot of care.' His voice was sombre
once more.

'May I meet him?' she asked.

He looked surprised, then shook his
head. 'I don't think that would be a
good idea.'

'Why not?' Amelia persisted. 'Are you
worried he might like me?'

She'd gone too far. Leo's face
darkened. 'Lucio is my son; he'll do
what his father commands. Whether he
likes you or not, it's my decision how I
protect him,' he growled.

Amelia's stomach flipped nervously.
He looked quite ferocious when he was
annoyed. His black brows drew
together and his eyes flashed. He
seemed larger in the room, an
overpowering animal presence. And yet
she instinctively felt there was no
physical threat from him. Not in anger,
at any rate.

She swallowed hard and decided then
to speak her mind. 'You appear to have
a lot of security in place. Surely the

nanny's job is to care for the child's needs? It goes without saying that there's a level of protection here from possible accidents and harm.'

Leo shook his head abruptly. 'I don't have to explain my reasons to you, Miss Knight. I know what Lucio needs.'

'And it isn't me,' Amelia finished for him, trying and failing to keep an edge of sarcasm out of her tone.

'I'm sorry,' Leo said, but his tone brooked no argument.

They finished their meal in silence, and Mrs Sorrento took away their plates and brought in dessert. There was nothing more to be said, Amelia thought in despair. She would never change this man's mind. What would she do? He would leave her at the airport in the morning, but she couldn't go home without a ticket. Could she find other work in Trinita? If not, she was stranded. A wave of panic caught in her throat. She gripped her cutlery until it passed.

There was a high-pitched wail from

somewhere in the house. Mora Sorrento came running in. 'Leo, it's Lucio. He's colicky again.'

Leo strode from the room with a brief apology to Amelia. She sat alone at the vast table for a moment. She had a choice: she could sit here on her own politely and wait for Leo and Mora to return, or she could risk Leo's wrath and go and help with the crying baby. She had five years' experience with young children and had nursed several babies prone to colic and night-time crying. One of her three charges in her previous job had been colicky on a regular basis. She knew she could soothe Lucio.

Amelia pushed her chair back. Before she could talk herself out of it, she moved fast. She followed the noise of a baby wailing, up the stairs and along a never-ending corridor until she came to a bedroom.

The door was open, and in a large pastel-blue cot a baby lay, his face red with distress. Leo was crouched beside him, talking urgently in a low voice.

'Could you please fetch a bottle of warm milk?' Amelia asked Mora calmly. Her heart was thudding. Would Leo let her tend to his child?

The older woman nodded and left swiftly. Amelia ignored Leo's thunderous look and picked the baby up from the cot mattress, talking to him in a soothing tone. 'Hello, Lucio. I'm Amelia. Let's get you more comfortable, shall we?'

Without a glance at Leo, but very aware of him, she worked quickly and efficiently, all the while murmuring gently to the baby. She checked that he wasn't damp, but his nappy seemed perfectly dry. She loosened his baby vest and let his legs wriggle free. Then she walked around the room, rocking him gently. When the crying stopped she lowered him to his mattress, and then opened the window to let a slow breeze circulate. It was still hot air, but better.

When Mora returned, Amelia took

the bottle, picked the baby up again and put the teat to his mouth. He sipped the milk, his big brown eyes on her, seeking reassurance. Beside her, Amelia could tangibly feel the bristling vibes from Leo. To his credit, he hadn't spoken his disapproval in front of his son. He didn't need to. Amelia was attuned uncannily to his mood. To Lucio, though, Leo spoke patiently and with obvious love. Lucio was a tiny version of his father, with a thick mop of raven hair and a sun-kissed copper complexion.

'That's better, isn't it?' Amelia said, more to herself than to the baby, as she handed the empty bottle back. 'Bad dreams and sore tummies disappear when we're cooler. The milk will help you get back to sleep.'

She stayed until Lucio's breathing became regular and he was fast asleep. Then she left him there with Leo and went downstairs to wait. She expected the lash of his fury, but Leo looked relieved when he joined her again.

There was a reluctant admiration in his eyes when he spoke. 'I think you proved your skills in there. Thank you. Lucio cries on a regular basis. It can take hours to settle him.'

'I didn't do it to prove my skills,' Amelia said, stung. Did he think her so calculating and cold-hearted?

'I apologise. I didn't mean it like that. I simply meant that you know what you're doing. Your experience of nannying comes through.'

'So you admit I'm a good nanny. Do I have the job, then?'

He swung away from her, the line of his back rigid as he paced the room. Eventually he turned to her again. Amelia tilted her chin to face him. Did he have to be so annoyingly tall? His broad shoulders loomed over her. But she was determined not to step back. She kept her gaze steady.

Leo's jaw tightened. He ran his fingers through his hair, leaving it sticking up and unruly. 'I'm sorry. You did a good job tonight. But you're too young, too slight in build. I need someone older and stronger.'

'I'm slight? What has that got to do with it?' Amelia asked in bewilderment. 'I'm hardly here to lift weights. Besides, I'm stronger than I look.'

'Are you really?' Leo asked dangerously.

Before Amelia could argue further, he had moved panther-fast and lifted her up. For a moment she was pressed against his chest. She felt its solid strength and the steady beat of his heart. She smelt his masculine scent, something unique — not a manufactured perfume or aftershave, but simply him. His warm breath brushed the top of her hair. As her body responded wildly, heat flooding through her, he placed her gently back on her feet. Was it her imagination, or did he look flushed too? His pupils were black, set against the golden irises. His lips curved in a satisfied smile.

'You see, Amelia, you're not so strong. In fact you're as light as a feather.'

She could protest. She could scream 'how dare you'. But she suspected Leo would only enjoy it all the more. So she forced herself to remain calm as an idea came to her.

'How long will it take you to advertise the job again and to read the résumés and organise interviews?' she asked calmly. Her heart thudded against her ribs, reluctant to let the feel of his body on hers go. She tried to ignore it.

He stepped away from her, letting the air between them settle. 'You don't give up, do you?' he said, shaking his head. 'The answer, sadly, is at least a few weeks. It takes time to coordinate the newspaper advertisements and responses. I prefer that Lucio has an English nanny, which is why we advertised in the London newspapers. This time I shall go personally to interview candidates.'

'In the meantime, why don't you let me stay, on a trial basis? Give me a few months to prove myself before you advertise. What do you say?' *Please*.

Mora had come to stand at the entrance to the room. She nodded to Leo.

He sighed. 'Very well, Amelia. You win. Three months' trial.' He started to leave but then turned back to her, his expression serious and an edge of steel in his voice. 'But this isn't a game. This is my son we're talking about. You can't fail me.'

Amelia quailed inwardly at his veiled threat. Outwardly she smiled her thanks. There was relief too — she had the job! She was used to the various and constant demands of three children in her care. How difficult could it be looking after just one?

★   ★   ★

Leo was in his study on the ground floor of the house. It was late at night, and Mora and Amelia had long since excused themselves. He had tiptoed

33

into Lucio's room to reassure himself that his son was there, safe and asleep. Now he stood at the window, looking out at the soft blackness beyond the high wall. Usually it was his favourite time and place. He loved the Trinita rainforest, the pulse of its heartbeat and the fantastic variety of its colourful wildlife woven within it. It was his home in all the ways that mattered. Normally he was at peace here. But not tonight.

Images of a diminutive blonde with serious grey eyes kept interrupting his calm. Why had he swept her up into his arms? It was madness. Yet he couldn't help but remember the feel of her soft skin against him. She had appeared in the forest like a ghost asking for his help. She was scared of the caiman. She'd freaked at the beetle. She didn't belong in a jungle setting, that was clear to him.

Yet she'd stood up to him and argued her case to stay. Her sea-grey eyes had turned to gunmetal as she held her ground. Why was she so desperate for this particular post? Why was she set on being Lucio's nanny? There were surely many such jobs in England to choose from. Leo tried to set aside his unease. He sat and opened a book, but the words wouldn't focus. With an impatient sigh he slammed the cover shut.

The most important thing was Lucio's safety. If Amelia turned out to be any threat at all, he'd have no compunction about throwing her out, or worse. He could hardly explain to her why security was so vital; his desire to keep his son safe. She would have to take it on trust.

He tensed suddenly. From upstairs came the telltale creak of floorboards. Someone was up and about. It was unlikely to be Mora, who never suffered from insomnia. He always had the house to himself after midnight.

Silently he moved from the study out into the hall and listened. There it was again. Somebody was walking on the storey above. Leo moved fast for a large man, and quietly. Years of tracking animals in the jungle had paid off. He grabbed her arm and spun her round. Amelia's face was white with shock. She gasped at him.

'What do you think you're doing?' he whispered savagely.

'I couldn't sleep. It's so hot in my room. I was trying to get some cool air, and then I thought I'd check on Lucio. Will you please let me go.' This last was said with an icy dignity, and he let her wrench her arm loose from his hard fingers.

He took a good look at her. Her pale blonde hair was loose and tousled, curling damply at her temples. She was wearing a pastel-blue nightdress that reached to her knees, revealing shapely legs and neat ankles. Was she aware that he could clearly see the outline of her breasts under the thin material? His body hardened at the sight of the peaks of her nipples. He suppressed a desire to rub the nub of his thumb across them, and averted his gaze.

What was he thinking of? She was now officially his son's nanny. As such, she was out of bounds. He had not been with a woman since Grace left. His body might miss the touch of a woman, but it could not be this particular woman. Besides, he didn't trust her. None of this appeared to matter to his wayward body, but it did to his principles.

She hugged her arms across her chest. So she had seen the direction of his thoughts. Too bad. Leo wanted answers. 'Didn't Mora show you how to work the air conditioning in your room?'

She went an even rosier shade of pink and shook her head. 'She showed me a switch, but I missed her saying what it was for. I was so tired after my long journey.' She yawned on cue and rubbed her face, looking even younger.

'I'll turn it on for you,' Leo said gruffly. 'It can be temperamental; it's an old system.' She let him lead the way to the guest bedroom.

The king-size bed looked as if a battle had been fought on it. The covers were flung about and the sheet twisted like a rope. Leo tried not to imagine her lying there, hot and damp. He focused on the air conditioning unit, checking it unnecessarily before showing her the switch and setting it going. It rattled to show it was working, and a blessed coolness seeped into the room.

Amelia sighed in relief. 'Thank you, that's marvellous. I'll sleep now. In fact, I feel like I could crash for twelve hours or so.'

'Lucio is an early riser,' Leo told her. 'I don't think you'll get the full twelve.'

'Oh, I didn't mean . . . of course I'll be up before him.' Amelia was flustered.

'I'm teasing you,' Leo said. 'Tomorrow you can start your new duties a little late. Mora will cope with Lucio's breakfast and entertainment. Sleep well.'

He was about to leave but glanced

back at the door. Amelia was already in the bed, covered in cotton sheets with only her head showing. She looked small and vulnerable and a little lonely. He ignored a sudden rush of sympathy. She might be all she said she was. Or she might not. He couldn't take any chances when it came to his son.

'Why were you going to check on Lucio so late at night?' he asked. But there was no answer. The shape in the bed rose and fell with even breaths. Amelia was fast asleep.

Leo went back to his study, his emotions turbulent. He tried to forget the shape of Amelia's body under her nightdress. He blocked the feel of her skin where he had touched her to lift her up and later to stop her progress to Lucio's room. Had he made a mistake letting her stay? Was she genuine? Would she really take good care of his son? Or was he repeating the mistake he'd made hiring the previous nanny? She was a woman who'd turned out to be lazy and incompetent but clever enough to cover it up, at least for a while, until he had realised her true colours.

The macaws were screeching their morning welcome over the forest canopy before Leo succumbed to sleep. He was finally able to rest, because he'd come to a decision regarding Miss Amelia Knight.

Despite his well-earned reputation as a recluse, Leo had vowed that for the few months of her employment at Grenville, he was going to keep Amelia firmly in his sights, even if it meant sticking to her side like thick forest honey.

3

Amelia woke late to strong, bright sunlight playing on her face. She threw back the covers, full of vigour. She had a job; she had her new beginning. She was determined to do it well. Leo would have no complaints. Leo. She flinched in embarrassment, remembering the previous night. She hadn't put a wrap around her nightdress, having been so overheated. Plus, she hadn't thought anyone would be awake so late.

The nightdress's flimsiness had cooled her, but it had also revealed far too much to Leo's dark gaze. She hesitated in her dressing. She suddenly couldn't bear to face him. Below in the house came a woman's laughter. Amelia gave herself a mental kick. *You can't hide here all day.* She buttoned her blouse and tucked it into her skirt, then slid on a pair of flat-heeled shoes, remembering Leo's comments about her footwear. There. She looked presentable and ready to be a nanny.

Leo was in the kitchen eating pancakes. She heard the click of the housekeeper's shoes somewhere outside through the open window.

'Good morning,' Amelia said, feeling Leo's attention lick her face and determined to be calm and not let him see the effect he had on her, or to shrink from him in overwhelming embarrassment. She hadn't been naked last night; she had been wearing a nightdress. Okay, a slightly see-through one. But still . . .

'Can I help? Do you want me to fry the next batch of pancakes?' she offered.

'Sit and eat.' Leo nodded. 'You should relax and eat a good breakfast before you start. You're too slim.'

So he had thought of her. Amelia was strangely touched by this gesture. Except she was too thin for his tastes, obviously. Not that it should matter. He was her boss, and that was all. Besides, she didn't like to be ordered to eat. She hesitated. The pancakes smelled good, though.

'Go ahead,' Leo said. 'I won't be joining you.'

She felt a sense of relief, chased by disappointment. 'Where are you going?'

'I have to make the rounds of the estate,' Leo explained. 'Every morning I drive out to check everything. I'll be back in an hour or so.'

'What do you check?' Amelia asked. She absent-mindedly bit into a pancake that he had slid onto a plate in front of her. It tasted as good as it smelt.

'There are always maintenance issues. I'll check that the water sluice is working, for one thing, and I'll check the perimeter walls. Also, of course, it's an excuse to see the wildlife.'

'Wildlife?' Amelia shuddered. 'If it's like the animals I encountered yesterday, you're welcome to them.'

Leo's lips curved into a half-smile. 'This place grows on you after a while.

43

Trust me. Now, have you found the nursery yet?'

Amelia put another hot, sweet pancake onto her plate and looked up at Leo questioningly.

'It's probably easier if Mora shows you later,' he said. 'Eat up first. That's an order.'

Her hand froze on her cutlery, although she had to admit the pancakes were delicious. She had spent too many years obeying William's commands. She hadn't come halfway across the world for yet someone else to tell her what to do.

'What's the matter? You don't like Mora's cooking?' Leo frowned in concern.

'No, it's not that. These are fantastic.' It seemed churlish not to eat them.

She was being foolish. It was so hard, changing her life. Every tiny incident was an obstacle. She prickled and resented any attempt to tell her what to do, even when it was in her own interests. She finished up her plate. If she kept eating like this, she'd soon pile on the pounds.

'Right,' Leo said, 'I must go now.' But he stood there watching her as though reluctant to leave her on her own. What was he thinking, that she'd snatch the family silver and escape through the jungle?

'Okay.' She nodded. 'See you later then.'

'Later,' he said firmly. It sounded like more of a threat than a promise.

Amelia deliberately didn't answer. She didn't know what his problem was right now, and she didn't need to. As soon as she'd finished breakfast, she had to start her duties. Looking after Lucio was her priority, not his father.

She didn't look up from her plate until he'd gone. Then it was as if all her muscles flopped. She hadn't realised how tense she had been in his presence; how very aware she was of his every move.

She refused to spend another second thinking about Leo Grenville. Instead, she went looking for the housekeeper.

*   *   *

'Come with me,' Mora beckoned. 'I'll show you the rooms where you can entertain Lucio.'

They went upstairs, where Mora showed Amelia the nursery. It was a bright room painted in blue and green, with a frieze of cartoon characters dado-fashion along the walls. There was a daybed with a mobile hanging over it, and shelves of colourful books and stacks of toy trucks and aeroplanes. A dartboard hung on the far wall.

'It's a very ... mature room for a baby,' Amelia said. 'The colours and toys remind me of a room more fit for a pre-schooler.' She flushed, having spoken without thinking. 'Sorry, I didn't mean to criticise.'

Mora smiled sadly. 'You're right, of course. This is the way Leo has decorated his son's room. Lucio is Leo's *bebe*. His baby boy. He wants everything perfect for him growing up. But he thinks to the future maybe a little too much. Leo is very . . . '

'Overprotective,' Amelia finished for her with a wry smile. 'Yes, I noticed. But why? Lucio seems like a healthy little boy. Apart from his colic, he doesn't look in need of wrapping in cotton wool.' She looked at the housekeeper.

'It's not my business to tell you,' Mora said gently. 'You must ask Leo why.' She turned briskly to tidy a scattering of toys from the floor, indicating clearly that the conversation was over.

* * *

It was early afternoon before Amelia was able to sit for a brief rest. The baby had been restless and was now sleeping, finally worn out. She was worn out too. She rested her head on her hand. Then, sensing a presence, she looked up. Leo leaned on the door frame, frowning at her.

'Is there a problem?' she asked quickly. Her heartbeat picked up. What was it that made the air thicken between them?

'No problem,' he replied, pushing his long legs from the door to walk into the nursery.

'Are you checking up on me?'

'Should I?' His amber gaze touched her hair and her body before catching her eyes and holding them.

Amelia flushed angrily. There was no denying the effect he had on her. A checklist of symptoms included a too-fast heartbeat, heated skin, and hyper-alert nerve endings. 'There's absolutely no need to,' she forced herself to say in a calm, cold tone at odds with the fever of her body. 'Lucio is perfectly fine with me. We've had an entertaining morning, and now he's having a short nap.' Her voice came out crystal clear, almost haughty.

'Entertaining?' Leo's laugh was unexpected. It was warm and deep and oh-so-magnetic; the kind of laugh that made her want to join in. *As if.* She reminded herself that he had been frowning when he watched her. What had been going through his head? She couldn't read him.

'My son is exhausting company,' Leo went on. '*Entertaining* is one way of describing it. You have your work cut out for you, Amelia.'

She heard the pride in his tone when he spoke of Lucio; heard how sweet her name sounded, rolling from his lips. 'I'm up to the challenge,' she said.

He quirked an eyebrow. 'Are you?' he said softly.

The room was suddenly too silent. It was as if Amelia's vision had narrowed until all she could see was Leo: his tall body, the broad shoulders and tapered waist, the length of him, and the strong muscles of his thighs visible under his faded work trousers. For a wealthy man, he didn't bother to show the trappings of it. He still looked like an estate worker. But a damned sexy one.

'What did you want?' she asked. She folded her arms and waited him out.

'I wondered if you wanted a ride into town. I'm going in now. It's an opportunity to get supplies. Mora will look after Lucio while we're out.'

Amelia hadn't realised her breath had been caught somewhere in her ribcage until she gave a sigh. Leo was back by the door. She had space between them. And that was a good thing, right? He was waiting for an answer. The dimple was back, a small crescent dip in his bristled cheek. He needed a shave. And to brush his hair. It was unruly, curling at his collar. There were dark hairs showing, too, where the shirt collar was unbuttoned.

A shaft of pure desire licked through her. It was unseemly. It was unwanted. It was . . . impossible to ignore.

'Amelia? Miss Knight?' He was mocking her silence.

'Yes, yes, thank you. Have I time to get ready?' She couldn't meet his gaze, but pretended to be busy closing the picture book lying on the table.

'Ten minutes. I'll meet you at the gates. Don't be late.'

★ ★ ★

She had the satisfaction of being ready before him. She was standing at the gates when the jeep drew up. He threw her a glance of approval as he opened the door of the vehicle for her. He'd changed into grey trousers and a white shirt, and had shaved. The clean line of his jaw showed. Amelia swallowed and concentrated on getting into the high seat of the jeep without tripping.

The gates opened with the control panel and the jeep made the turn onto the dirt road. She clung to the door handle as it rocked. Leo's grip on the steering wheel was light and confident. He glanced briefly over at her. 'Don't worry, it gets smoother. The road's surfaced further on.'

'I'm fine, really.'

'And that's why your hand's welded to that handle?'

'It's not. Okay, so I'm not used to off-road driving,' she muttered.

That deep laugh again. 'This isn't off-road, Amelia. Believe it or not, this is one of the better roads around here.'

'I can believe it,' she snapped as her stomach lurched over a pothole. She grabbed at her seat with her other hand and got Leo's arm instead. It was warm and solid. She let go as if it were on fire. 'Sorry,' she said.

'Relax. We're perfectly safe.'

I'm not safe. Not safe at all. I'm trapped in a small space with a man who turns my senses upside down. She bit at her lip. When she dared to look up, she saw Leo frowning at her before he stared back out at the road.

'So why did you come here? Why does a city girl like you run away to the jungle?' he asked.

There was no way she was answering that. To distract him, she asked her own question. 'Why do you have Lucio's room fixed up as if he's much older?'

For a moment she thought she'd gone too far. The air inside the jeep stilled like an approaching storm. But when he answered, his voice was calm. Steady. Controlled. 'Just how long have you been caring for my son? One morning. You think that's sufficient to give you the right to question my fathering skills?'

'I'm not saying you're a bad father,' she said quickly, 'but Lucio's only a baby. His nursery is more fit for an older child. With Lucio's baby energy he needs a soft rug for playing with, a mobile, a chew ring, a cloth teddy. I don't know; there's lots of things I can think of. But instead he's got a dartboard and a box full of plastic toy cars. It's as if you want him to grow up too quickly.'

She stopped. She'd said too much. Leo didn't answer. She risked a glance. His jaw was tightened and a tiny pulse was visible.

'Perhaps your ex-wife . . . ' Amelia

trailed off. She suddenly realised she had no idea about his ex-wife. She'd assumed the ex-Mrs Grenville lived on the island somewhere. Now, by the look on Leo's face, she'd stepped way over the mark.

'My ex-wife,' Leo said, pronouncing the words bitterly, 'had as much idea about raising a child as that parrot in the palm tree over there.' The colourful bird flew up in front of the jeep as he spoke.

'I thought maybe . . . ' Amelia started.

'You thought maybe Lucio's suffering by living with his father. Maybe he should be with his mother.' Leo's voice cut across her, tight with anger.

'I'm sorry,' she said.

The jeep shook as it drove fast over a low bridge, brushing the shiny vegetation on the door window. 'Let me be the judge of what my son needs. Not you.' Leo's voice now was cold, cutting her out.

'Don't you think a fresh perspective

can be helpful?' she tried again. 'As his nanny, I have an interest in his upbringing. Is it possible he's missing his mother, and that's why he cries? Babies have an instinct for when their parents are close by.'

Leo's shoulders slumped and he took one hand from the wheel to rub his forehead. Then he pulled the vehicle to the verge and stopped the engine. 'He'll get over Grace, believe me. He can hardly remember her. He was only three months old when she left. She's been gone three months. And before you ask, no she isn't on Trinita. She left us and went back to England.'

'Your wife was English?'

'As English as you are. Blonde hair, blue eyes, and tender skin that hated the sun. I was a fool to bring her here. This is a difficult climate. You have to be born to it.' The anger had gone from his voice; instead he sounded bleak. Then with a conscious effort he lifted his shoulders and nodded towards the windscreen. 'We've arrived.'

The marketplace was busy. Leo left Amelia at a stall selling leather goods and went to order petrol. He saw her pale blonde hair as she mingled with the crowds and cursed under his breath. What was it about her? He'd known many women, and Amelia Knight wasn't special. So why did those big grey eyes have such an effect on him? Why did her questions rile him?

Because she didn't know what she was talking about. Didn't know that Grace was a topic that was out of bounds. He felt an unwelcome admiration for her. He'd growled at her and pretty much told her to butt out from how he brought up his son. Yet she'd persisted, to the extent he wanted to lean over and kiss her mouth shut!

He didn't have any feelings left for Grace; they had withered with what she'd done. But he didn't want her name mentioned. Lucio should never be reminded of his mother as he grew up. And he didn't want to be reminded of his ex-wife either, who had deserted them both.

Leo sighed. He didn't actually need petrol. He'd made up the excuse to visit the town so he could see Amelia alone. She was hiding something, and he had to find out what. Who was she? Why had she travelled so far for one job?

He hadn't reacted well to her comments about Lucio. He knew he was overprotective of his son, but he had his reasons. Amelia didn't need to know them. And if he were honest, wasn't he just a little bit put out that she could so calmly soothe the baby, when he himself was helpless to know what to do? He put that thought to one side.

He ordered the petrol and found his way back to the market, then searched the crowd for her. There she was, her head bent in conversation with another woman at a stall. There was a bulging bag of fruit beside her. She looked up as he approached. For an unguarded moment he was treated to the brightness of her smile. Then she realised it was him. The smile vanished. It was as if the sun had gone behind the clouds.

'Are you ready to go?' he asked her.

She lifted up the bag of fruit in answer. 'Yes. I've bought out the market!'

'You don't have to buy food. Mora does the housekeeping.' He was aware of how clipped his tone was, and unfriendly. But he couldn't help it; he was on edge, and unsure. He wanted to pick her up and shake it out of her. *Who are you? What do you want?* Or perhaps, if he were honest with himself, was it because she had riled him by arguing about Lucio?

'I know, but they were impulse buys,' she was saying. 'I haven't seen some of these fruits before, and I'd like to try them.'

There was a dancing spark in her grey eyes. It tugged at him. It hinted at a sense of fun; of anticipation — things he hadn't experienced for an age. He was suddenly envious of her. 'Come with me,' he said.

Her face flashed annoyance at his order.

'Please,' he amended.

'Where to?' Amelia asked, still not following, her hands on her waist — challenging him.

He sighed. 'Amelia, is it so very difficult just to come with me across the square for a drink?'

'Why didn't you say so, instead of barking at me?'

'I wasn't barking.' His own annoyance rose at her prickliness.

'Really?'

'Yes, really. Forget the drink,' he growled.

Her hands swung loose from her waist. She grabbed her bag and closed the gap between them. 'I'm sorry Leo,' she said. 'I . . . Look, can we try that conversation again?'

He smelt her fragrance all of a sudden — a sweet scent of violets. It was out of place, like green English meadows, and contrasted with the heavy tropical aromas around them — ripe, exotic fruits, thick vines, and always the humid heat.

'Leo?' she said softly.

'It was only a drink. You looked so hot.' *Great choice of words*, he thought wryly. She did look hot, but not because of the searing afternoon sun. Hot — but out of bounds. His whole world was his son. This woman was here for a reason, and it wasn't for his needs.

'I'd love a drink.'

'There, was that so difficult?' he teased as they sat in the shade with two tall glasses in front of them.

'I have a problem with being told what to do.' She twisted her mouth.

'That's not a good trait in an employee,' he responded, trying for a light tone.

She glanced at him uncertainly and he smiled to show he wasn't serious. She visibly relaxed.

'No, perhaps not. I won't let it

interfere with my job. You don't need to worry about that.'

'Perhaps I should worry about other things,' he couldn't help remarking.

'Like what?' She sat up straighter. Her fingers tightened on the glass. He noted how slender they were. What would her touch feel like? The thought rose up out of nowhere. Annoyed with it, he spoke sharply. 'Like, what do I know about you?'

'You know everything that's on my résumé.'

'I know what you've written there.'

'What exactly are you saying? That I lied? That I made up my qualifications?' Her voice quivered and she looked ready to spring up out of her chair.

'I'm saying that I don't know you. That you're here on my island, in my house, caring for my son. But you could be anyone.'

'Why employ me then?'

Because my son needs a nanny. Because I can't trust anyone, so it might as well be you. Because Mora

61

chose you, and I trust her. Leo didn't say any of this. He couldn't tell her the truth. He didn't want to revisit the past.

'You need to prove I can trust you,' he said harshly. 'A good place to start is with your family. Who are you, Amelia?'

She stood up abruptly. 'Thank you for the drink. I'm ready to go back to the house now.'

He stood, too, and caught her arm. 'Not so fast.' He spun her round to face him. Her face reached his chest. Her skin was perfect, her grey eyes thickly lashed; and her mouth cried out to be kissed. He had to fight against leaning down to do so. The physical pull was intense. Her lips parted to show perfect, neat white teeth. He groaned silently, and his body hardened. All his nerves shrieked *mistake*. It was difficult to let her go.

He stepped back. For a moment she was still, and her eyes sought his. They were darkened, and there was a faint flush on her cheeks. He knew she felt it too, this attraction between them.

Hadn't it been there from the instant he saw her appear in the jungle clearing? The memory of the soft feel of her skin where he'd lifted the beetle . . . This was madness! He had Lucio to think of and had to focus on what was important.

'You haven't answered me,' he said, his throat raw.

'I'll prove to you that you can trust me,' Amelia said quietly, never losing his gaze. 'I *will* do that. You promised me a three-month trial, and I'll use it to show you who I am.'

'And I have to be content with that?' His sarcasm was thickly laid on.

Her whole body stiffened, and he knew he'd angered her. Briefly, he wondered if he'd lost her. Would she resign? But why should that matter to him?

When her answer came, it was as if she had torn it from some deep place within. 'My father . . . my father is William Knight.'

4

Amelia felt sick. Her hands shook as if with a fever. She waited for the inevitable expression of admiration to appear on Leo's face, but it didn't come.

'Are we talking about William Knight, CEO of the Knight Banking Corporation?'

'The very same.' Her words were glued to her tongue. There was a pause, during which she kept her eyes downcast. She interlaced her fingers; gripped her knuckles; didn't breathe. When he didn't speak, she looked up. His face was unreadable.

'Go on,' she said, 'tell me how marvellous my father is. What a wonderful, strong, forceful character. How successful a businessman.' Now she breathed. In and out. Too fast.

Then he said softly, 'How did you

know I've met your father?'

She shivered. He didn't move but she sensed his power, coiled. She had blown her cover. 'I saw an article about you in a business magazine. You were meeting my father in London last year.'

'So you chose to come here. It wasn't a random job.' His voice was quiet but deadly.

'It wasn't deliberate,' Amelia protested. 'It was a coincidence. I . . . I had to leave London, and then there was the advert for the nanny position. I saw the name Grenville and I knew who you were.'

'How very convenient.'

She risked a glance at him. His amber eyes were dark, his jaw strongly defined. He was gritting his teeth, and it was clear he was restraining himself. She drew back. At that, he put up his hands as if in surrender.

'Look, if I accept that you're telling me the truth, what then?'

'It *is* the truth. I had to leave, and the position here was a wonderful gift.'

'What were you running from?' Leo asked bluntly. 'Your father?' Amelia gasped, and Leo smiled drily. 'How did you describe him — ? Strong, forceful and successful. Yes, I'd say he had all those qualities. But I'd also guess he'd be impossible to live with. Am I right?'

She lifted the bag of fruit and fumbled with the handle, hoping Leo would give up. But he didn't, even when she began to walk away from the market, blindly heading in the direction of the jeep — she hoped.

He walked beside her, his longer legs easily keeping stride. Agitation made her stumble. Leo caught her and held her for a heartbeat longer than necessary. Then he set her from him and put a finger under her chin, gently. 'It will help to talk,' he said.

'Yes, I was running away from him,' she blurted out. 'I wanted to get to the furthest corner of the world.'

Somehow they'd reached the jeep. Leo took the heavy bag of fruit, and then Amelia was huddled on the passenger seat. Her words were tumbling out like a waterfall.

'I was given every advantage an only child of rich parents could have, including a hothouse education. My mother died when I was ten, and William sent me away to boarding school. He had high hopes for me. I was to join the family business, you see. I was his heir.'

'But you had your own ideas,' Leo said.

'I've always loved children. I wanted to be a nanny. William was very against it, but eventually he agreed to pay for my college studies. I think he thought I'd get fed up with it and then I'd come round to what he wanted.'

'But that didn't happen,' Leo guessed.

She was glad in a weird way that he was there. It was as if the words were like poison leaching from her. The more she spoke, the better she felt. She'd held it all in for so long. Leo's solid presence was comforting. Well, maybe that was the wrong word, she corrected herself. She was too aware of him to call it comfort. Her body was too attuned to his.

'No, it didn't. I love being a nanny. I love the responsibility, and the reward of seeing my children flourish. My father — William — is very controlling. Eventually it was easier to leave.' She turned to Leo, needing him to understand. 'I want to live my own life, in my way.'

'So when I asked you to come with me for a drink, you thought I was trying to control you?' he asked.

'It sounded like an order.' She smiled shakily. 'I can't help it. I bristle when I'm ordered about.'

He nodded. The corner of his mouth quirked as if he understood.

Wanting to break the sudden silence, Amelia joked shakily, 'If you hadn't been so bossy about the drink, none of this would've come out.'

'Bossy?' He raised an eyebrow and appeared to consider before replying,

'You could be right. I know my own mind. And I am master of my house.' It was a blunt, honest reply.

Master of Grenville House. Amelia looked out the window at the scenery flying by. They were driving back now to that very house, Leo's land and property. She had felt close to him there while telling her story. But was he domineering, too? Had she leapt from the frying pan into the fire? She remembered that she could leave. If it all got too much, she'd go. So why did it hurt to think of leaving Leo?

'Your sandals,' Leo said, surprising her. 'Where are they?'

'In the rubbish bin. You were right, they were incredibly impractical.' Not to mention incredibly battered and misshapen from their journey through the undergrowth.

'They made you feel good. That's what you told me.'

'I bought them the day I left home. I was taking my stuff to a friend's apartment to stay, and I walked by the shop and there they were.' The awful way she'd left William and her home flooded back.

'You parted on bad terms?'

'Very,' Amelia said with feeling. 'He promised that if I left, he'd see to it that I never worked in England as a nanny again. I believe him. He has many, many business contacts. It'll be easy for him.'

She thought she heard Leo swear under his breath. But he said nothing, and then they were through the gates of Grenville House.

* * *

The swimming pool was built into the white-stoned patio. Brightly coloured plastic inflatable lilos floated on the surface of the turquoise water. It looked cool and inviting after the dusty drive back from town; a place where Amelia could hide and pretend she had never told Leo about William and her life in London. With a bright smile, she rummaged in her suitcase looking for her swimsuit.

Lucio was happy in his bouncy chair in the kitchen while Mora prepared a meal. Surely Leo wouldn't mind if she took a quick dip in the pool. But what if he wanted to join her? Amelia's stomach flipped, and her treacherous heart joined in. Just the image of Leo in swimming gear was enough to trigger it. She gulped, realising she'd have to change into her summer bikini. Why, oh why hadn't she packed her old sports swimsuit instead?

When she went downstairs, she found that Leo had had the same brilliant idea for getting rid of the afternoon heat. He was in the swimming pool, and gave the impression of being relaxed.

He swam a length lazily, not yet seeing Amelia emerge from the house, and mulled over what had happened earlier. She promised that he could trust her. But could he? She hadn't seen fit to mention that she knew of the

71

connection between him and her father. She'd only told him who she was because he'd pressed her on it.

His muscles tense, Leo switched to a fast crawl. The physical burn felt good. He sliced through the water, but his speed-swim failed to dislodge Amelia from his brain.

He couldn't make her out. She hated authority, yet was desperate to be in his employment. She appeared to dislike wildlife, yet had chosen a tropical island abundant in it to relocate to. There was no doubt she loved children, having seen her deal with Lucio's crying. Yet there was no hint of an established boyfriend or ex with whom she might plan a family of her own.

That last thought was stray. Leo dived with vigour. He didn't care if she had a lover or not. It was immaterial. All he had to do was remember that. He was attracted to her. He didn't deny it. But he was strong enough to ignore that.

He surged out of the water for a

breath and then forgot to take it. Amelia stood tentatively at the end of the pool. She was wearing a crimson bikini that barely covered her curves. His body forgot the idea of ignoring her, and he sent up a silent thanks as she slipped into the water. If he'd had to watch her further . . . He plunged back underwater to cool off.

When he came back to the surface, she was chasing a plastic lilo that flipped as she grabbed it. It gave Leo a moment to assess her. With her hair slickly wet, she looked younger; vulnerable. The things she'd told him about her life with her father came back. The man sounded like a domineering fool. What kind of father sent his grieving child away to boarding school? He couldn't imagine parting with Lucio. Even the image of it sent pain slicing into him. He might not be coping too well, but he'd never be without his boy. How could Grace bear to have let him go? He never would.

His chest tight with that vow, he

stared at Amelia. Lucio's new nanny might look alluring with her big grey eyes, blonde curls, and scattering of freckles across her cheekbones, but what was underneath? What other secrets was she hiding from him?

He had been a sympathetic listener to her story. Having met William Knight, it sounded entirely plausible. He hadn't liked the man one bit when he met him in London. He came across as arrogant and sneering. If her story were true, then Amelia had done the right thing by fleeing across the world to find work. And if it wasn't?

Amelia's peal of laughter rang out over the shimmering pool. Her head was flung back and her hair shone in the sun. The lilo had a life of its own. The more she attempted to grab it, the more it bounced away from her across the pool's surface. Then, as he watched, she managed to grip it and lie back in the sunshine.

Amelia had no idea why Leo was scowling at her. Before she noticed it, she was the happiest she'd been in ages. She loved water, and this swimming pool was divine. The aquamarine liquid was warm and clean, and the sunshine sparkled on its surface. The chase for the lilo was ridiculous and tugged at her sense of fun. For once, she wasn't thinking of the past or fretting over the future. She simply was there.

Glancing over at Leo to invite him to join her had spoiled it. He was still glaring at her. Taken aback, she pretended not to notice. She wasn't going to let Leo's odd mood spoil this early-evening haven.

Why was he so angry, anyway? She swam away from him, using her hands to paddle the inflatable. There was a heaviness in her stomach. Of course — she shouldn't have told him so much. He probably despised her for running away. Hadn't he admitted he admired William's qualities? Why should she be surprised if Leo took her father's side?

Or maybe Leo was harking after the

older, stronger nanny he had demanded. She didn't understand why. On impulse, she slipped from the lilo into the water and turned to swim back. She'd ask him!

What she wasn't prepared for was that Leo had emerged to sit on the tiled edge of the pool. He was watching her like a cat. But her breath caught for a different reason. There was a trail of dark hair that ran from his muscular chest to his stomach. The sheer maleness of him made her blink. Raw desire rippled through her. His swimming shorts weren't brief, but her imagination took over. His thighs were strongly muscled. And she didn't dare speculate on the part of him between his hips and thighs. She looked away, her throat constricted. For a moment she forgot why she'd turned in that direction.

There was no escape now. There was simply Leo and her in the pool. An image of the lethal animal that had blocked her path when she arrived flashed in her mind. This felt similar. To get out using the steps, she had to pass him close enough to touch. Or instead, she could swim a length to avoid him and use the opposite set — which would look really foolish, as if she were afraid of him.

She tilted up her chin. He evoked many sensations in her, but fear wasn't one of them. Mora had said his bark was worse than his bite, and Amelia was pretty sure that was true. Now she was going to test it.

'Why were you staring at me?' she asked him.

He raised an eyebrow slowly and his gaze slid across her like warm honey. It raised goose bumps on her skin. 'You must be used to admiring stares when you wear that bikini,' he replied with a smile. It had a wolfish quality that she shied away from, uncertain now what she'd begun.

'Admiring stares, sure,' she agreed with a confidence that was entirely fabricated. She forced a light smile.

'But not angry ones. You weren't admiring me, you were censuring me.'

'Why would I need to do that?' His voice was low, his gaze penetrating hers as if he could read her mind.

She was annoyed with herself. She'd revealed more personal detail than she'd wanted to that afternoon in the jeep to him. She wanted to be judged on her performance as Lucio's nanny, not on her sad life prior to the island. This irritation coloured her voice as she snapped back, 'I have no idea. You told me I wasn't old enough or strong enough for the job. Maybe you were recalling that?' He looked taken aback. So she hadn't hit the nail on the head. What, then, had made him scowl?

'If you are what you say you are — ' His tone suggested the jury was still out. ' — then yes, I'd prefer an older woman in charge of my only son.'

The word 'only' was emphasised. She got it: she knew how precious his son was to him, and didn't need it spelt out. Any child in her charge got her full attention, whoever they were, whoever their parent was. Her anger flared. He didn't believe in her skill as a nanny.

'And stronger, of course,' she mocked, 'to fight off the enemies.'

His face blanched. She'd hit a nerve and she had no idea why. She opened her mouth to offer an apology, but Leo cut in.

'You have no idea what you're talking about. You think this is a game? What if I'm away from the house and there's an emergency? Could you deal with it? Can you protect him, lift him to safety and bar the door?'

Bar the door against what? 'If you have so little faith in me, why did you let me have the job?' she asked in frustration. The pool water eddied around her as she moved.

'You know why. I have no choice until your replacement gets here.'

'My replacement?' Amelia's voice rose. 'You promised me a three-month trial.'

Leo shook his head. She waited but

he didn't reply. There were fine lines around his mouth, which tautened.

'Leo?' she whispered.

'I'm sorry,' he said. 'I can't take the chance.'

'You can't take the chance that I'll be good at this? What's wrong here? Why won't you tell me?'

'Because . . . ' He pushed a hand through his wet hair in exasperation.

'Because you don't trust me,' Amelia finished for him. Her voice was flat. The pool water felt cold and her damp bikini uncomfortable.

'Because you haven't been here long enough for me to trust you,' he corrected.

Before she could move, he slid into the water beside her. She shivered. The sun was lowering and the temperature dropping. The goose bumps were back. Was it the cool air, or Leo's closeness?

'You'll still have your three months,' he said eventually. 'Lucio . . . seems to like you.'

Do you *like me?* The question flew to

her lips and hovered there, unuttered. 'Is that so difficult to admit?' she asked instead.

He looked abashed. She slipped past him to climb the steps out of the pool, very conscious of him behind her. She wished once more she didn't own such a skimpy outfit.

'Amelia.'

He was out now too. She turned and angled her face up to his. What was he going to say now? Hadn't he said enough? She took her towel and draped it over her shoulders. She felt safer with its thick softness between her and the air.

At that moment a monkey jumped from the outside foliage onto the top of the wall and screeched at them. Amelia nearly screeched back. Her heart pounded. The animal chattered as if laughing at her, then jumped away and vanished into the jungle.

Leo gave her a slow smile. Despite her anger with him, she felt herself respond with her own smile. Whatever trouble there was between them, he had the power to engage her senses, her reflexes. It troubled her. It was too much like control. He might be unaware of it, but she wasn't. And she didn't like it one little bit.

'I'd advise you not to leave the compound. That little guy has plenty of friends. They're inquisitive, and they have sharp teeth. In fact, they can be quite a nuisance if there's food around.'

'Not leave the compound? What, never?' She was astounded.

'Of course you can leave it, but it's best if you tell me in advance so I can drive you into town or wherever you wish to go. You shouldn't go walking alone.'

A little flicker of rebellion sparked in her. What was the problem with going outside the estate wall? What harm could come from it? It felt like she'd left one prison at her father's house in London only to land in another here on the island. If Leo didn't like her going outside, then too bad. She wasn't obliged to obey him.

5

It was a few days before Amelia got her chance. She got up early and went through to get Lucio up for the day. He gurgled and waved his arms as she dressed him. She picked him up and sang as she took him downstairs for breakfast.

Mora was already in the kitchen preparing the food. 'Good morning to you both. Would you like pancakes today?' She smiled.

'Just an egg, thank you. Shall I make it once I've fed this boy and put him in his bouncy chair?'

'Good idea,' the housekeeper said. 'Actually, that would be a big help, because I need to get ready to go into town. I'm visiting my sister today.'

'She lives in the town?' Amelia asked with interest as she got a bowl and began to whip the eggs.

'No, she lives with her family up in the foothills, so it's a bit of a journey. But I can catch the mountain bus in the town square,' Mora explained. 'Leo will take me in; he's got business today in town. Will you be all right all day on your own?'

'On my own? I'll be looking after Lucio; that will keep me busy.'

'Sorry, I didn't explain very well. Leo is taking Lucio to visit his grandparents today, so you won't be needed until this evening.'

'Oh. Right.' Amelia wasn't quite sure for a moment whether she was glad of the free time or not. 'Is Leo coming for breakfast?' She held up the egg box. 'Shall I cook more?'

Mora shook her head. 'He's eaten. Don't expect to see him; it's a busy day, so he won't be back until late.'

Amelia's spirits flattened. Leo had kept out of her way since their conversation in the pool. She'd seen him from a distance, working on the plantation with the men. For some reason he was never far from her mind. Okay, scratch that. She knew why. She was hypersensitive to his presence; fighting a deepening physical attraction to the man.

It will help to talk. His words when she'd let slip about who she was. Had she imagined a tenderness then? He hadn't interrupted as she let it all out. He'd been a reassuring presence in the enclosed space of the jeep. For a brief interlude they'd been close to each other — hadn't they? She'd never told anyone else about William's high-handedness. But then Leo had been angry with her in the pool. She hadn't imagined that, even if she couldn't fathom what she'd done. He'd deliberately widened the mental space between them until the moment in the jeep might never have occurred.

Mora appeared with her bags in the doorway. 'So I'll say goodbye. I've left your lunch and dinner prepared, and I'll see you tomorrow.'

'You're staying away overnight?' Amelia

hadn't thought of that. Her stomach plummeted as she realised she'd be alone with Leo that evening. Not alone, she corrected. Lucio would be upstairs asleep. The maids and estate workers would be on the grounds in their flat-roofed houses. She swallowed. She'd pretty much be alone with him. A tingle of dark excitement shot along her spine. She forced herself to concentrate on Mora and said goodbye.

From the window she watched Leo and Mora depart. Leo glanced once back up at her, then the vehicle shot off fast through the gates and vanished up the road. The house was suddenly quiet.

The morning passed slowly. Amelia tidied up in the kitchen, then did her own room, which took no time at all as she had so few possessions. Then she wandered into the nursery to see what she could do there. Nothing. It was neat and tidy.

Restlessly, she stepped across the floor of the nursery and went to look out the window. Beyond the tall white walls there was a sea of green leaves, and occasional rainbow-coloured birds flew up.

Leo's warning about the monkeys came back. Her mouth twisted wryly. Why was he never far from her thoughts? It was crazy to miss him when she'd hardly seen him since her arrival here. Besides, he'd be back later. They'd eat dinner together. She rather dreaded that, but thrilled at it too. How mixed up was she?

'I could have a picnic out there,' she said out loud, then stopped. Why not? Hadn't she promised herself she'd do it? She shrugged. How difficult was it? She'd take some food that Mora had left and go on a walk along the path. It wouldn't take more than an hour, and would rub off her boredom and allow her some freedom too. Hovering on the edge of that, not clearly defined, was an urge to prove Leo wrong. He'd made it clear he thought she was incapable of coping with the island climate and wildlife. What had he said — ? You have to be born to it. His ex-wife hadn't been, and she'd left. Well, Amelia would do better. She'd show him that being petite wasn't a negative. The thought grew horns.

Before she could argue her way back out of it, she headed downstairs. Her mood lifted. This was okay. It was going to be a fun afternoon. She imagined relating it to Leo over dinner and seeing his expression of approval. She'd do a lot to see his amber eyes warm to her. That made her face heat. Leo. Leo. She had it bad.

★ ★ ★

The forest closed over Amelia like a natural ceiling. She planted her feet firmly on the path. Each breath was warm and humid. The background buzz of animal noises was never-ending. The rucksack with her picnic was hot and clammy on her back. She was suddenly unsure if it was a good idea after all. What if the crocodile was on the path further up?

A white cockatoo landed on a branch nearby. It raised its sulphur-coloured crest comically. She laughed and her shoulders relaxed. As long as she stuck to the path, it would be fine. She would walk a bit more and then find a place to sit and eat. At any sign of a croc, she'd simply take a fast u-turn home.

Glad to have sorted that out, Amelia took a step forward. The cockatoo flew from branch to branch above her, and peered down with a cocked head. She grinned at it. There, what was so difficult? She was in the jungle, away from the house, and all was well. She made good progress along the well-maintained surface.

'Shall I picnic here?' she asked the cockatoo as they reached a glade. A thick ray of sun played on it. Butterflies flitted in the column of light. She was entranced. This was so different to her first impression of the jungle. She'd been scared the day she arrived; fearful of William's wrath when he discovered where she'd gone; terrified of the alien world she'd landed in. Then she'd met Leo. Her skin tingled at the memory of his touch on her skin.

She waved away an errant fly. Her forehead was damp with sweat. From nowhere inside her there was a brief flare of fear. She forced herself to concentrate on the comical bird and the dancing butterflies. She was still entranced — wasn't she? But William had done too good a job of scraping away at her confidence, whittling it down with his cold words and disparaging tone. Suddenly she knew it was a mistake coming here. She wasn't equipped for the jungle. What did she know about it? Nothing. She was way out of her comfort zone.

'Stop it!' she cried, pushing her hands to either side of her head, trying to blot out his voice in her thoughts. 'I can do this. I *will* do this. I'm not going to let him win. This is *my* life now. And I am capable of living it.'

She put her foot forward. There was no way she was going back to the house without having had her picnic. She gripped the handles of the rucksack, almost pulling her body on against its will.

She walked along for a while. The landscape changed, and the path was now of beaten earth rather than tarmac. She frowned, trying to think what else was different. She'd started at the plantation near the house. The jungle was *thinner* here, somehow. There were fruit and coffee trees, and cleared patches where the workers had hacked at the vegetation. Here the trees clung close together, their fleshy leaves entwined with hanging vines. The smell of damp earth was thicker. The forest birds clamoured. With panic, Amelia wondered how far she'd come from the house.

'I should go back,' she murmured. 'This is too far. I'll go and eat back there at the glade.'

Then she saw it — a wide gap in the

trees with a rocky wall on the far side. A stream of water cascaded down its surface into a green pool below. It was perfect.

★ ★ ★

She was feeling smug. That was the only word for it. She lay back on the thin raffia picnic mat with pleasure. The rucksack gaped open, its contents eaten. On the way back she'd only have the roll of mat and the empty drinks flask to carry in it.

So much for the Trinita climate. It wasn't so bad, Amelia decided. Yes, it was humid, and there were a few too many flies. But hey, there were worse places to live. If Leo gave her the post after the three months were up, she'd definitely stay.

She sat up and hugged her arms, holding that delicious idea. She'd never have to face William or London again. She'd enjoy looking after Lucio. She'd enjoy . . . seeing Leo every day. She lowered her chin onto her arms, musing. She found him very attractive. Was it mutual? She sighed. Hard to tell. And so what if it was? It couldn't come to anything. She needed the work. And even if it was mutual, it wouldn't work out, she just knew it. A sick feeling rose up as she remembered how her previous relationships had ended, every one of them. Maybe it was inevitable that this one, if it developed, would go the same way.

A fat drop of rain struck her head, interrupting her. It was quickly joined by a shower of them. She shrieked as the heavens opened. In moments, the rain was coming down in sheets. The rainy season — Leo had described it, and warned her that it was coming. Well, it was here now. Her hair was plastered to her skull and her eyes streamed as if with tears. Her clothes were soaked.

Through a wall of rain, she saw with alarm that the waterfall had swollen. The green pool was expanding rapidly.

The earth beneath her was slick. Rivulets snaked across its surface, moving twigs and leaves fast. Now the soil was sheer mud, black and sticky. It sucked at her feet.

She grabbed for the sodden rucksack, the rain drumming on her back as she bent to shut the bag's flap. She put it on awkwardly. It snagged on the wet material of her shirt. Her fingers were slippery.

She had to get away from the pool. Half-sliding in mud and new rivers, she sought the path. It was there, wasn't it? She'd come in between those trees. But when she got there, the way was blocked with fallen trunks. Disorientated, she turned back.

No sense of direction, Amelia. That's your problem. Of course you can't cope with this. You shouldn't have left London. What were you thinking? Was it her own voice, or that of William? She almost gave in to it; agreed with it. She could have slumped there in self-pity, waiting to be rescued, giving in to whatever fate demanded.

But out of nowhere a steely thread appeared deep in her stomach. She was an adult. She had to take charge. Her heart rattled in her chest. She was way out of her comfort zone now. What would Leo do? There was more than a pang of regret that she hadn't listened to him and stayed inside the mansion's grounds. Idiot! What had she proved, really? That she was incompetent. *Pathetic*, she railed at herself.

She was the only one who could get herself safely home. She pushed down the sudden yearning for Leo — his quiet strength; his dark golden eyes; his broad shoulders that could carry her out of here.

The ground beneath her was now dangerously soft and submerged, like a shallow sea. The path had gone. She was abruptly calm. She knew what to do. There was a narrow ledge in the rock. It was safely clear of any rise in the water below.

She took a step, thinking to climb up

to it. Instead, her foot caught in the slime and she fell heavily. There were branches. She heard a crack as her ribs connected with the wood; heard her own frightened cry. Then nothing . . .

* * *

Leo's brows drew together as the house receded out of view. Beside him, in the passenger seat, Mora Sorrento sent him a sympathetic smile. Lucio was strapped safely into his car seat in the back.

'Have I done the right thing, employing her?'

'You have Lucio with you today, but we can't be with the baby twenty-four seven,' the housekeeper said sensibly. 'At some point, you have to trust someone else with his care.'

'A stranger?' He slammed his hand on the steering wheel, annoyed by his own indecision. He had a strong urge to spin the wheels and drive fast back to the house. There he could shake the truth out of Amelia and find out what she really wanted; why she was here. How well she treated his son when no one was looking.

'She's not a stranger,' Mora said gently. 'I know she's only been with us a few days, but I've been observing her with him. She's good with the child. He likes her.'

Leo blew out a breath. His son wasn't the only one who liked her. He was beginning to like Amelia Knight a little too much himself. It was why he'd been avoiding her the last few days. The image of her dressed in that bikini; her big grey eyes that projected all her emotions; the slenderness of her that made him want to encircle her waist with his hands and lift her up so his lips could reach hers . . . It was a kind of craziness. He desired a woman whom he didn't trust. History was repeating itself — except it wouldn't. He wouldn't go there; couldn't bear to repeat the pain.

'She isn't Grace,' Mora spoke softly.

Leo squeezed the wheel, feeling the pressure build under his fingers. He relaxed them deliberately. 'You haven't forgotten what we've been through this year. Tell me that lightning doesn't strike twice in the same place.'

'I haven't forgotten,' Mora said. 'Grace . . . has a lot to answer for. She's broken all our hearts. But you're a good father. You're doing your best for your son.'

'Am I?' he asked darkly. 'I don't know if I am. I'm not sure I know what the best is for Lucio. Or whether I'm providing it.'

'But you have to move on. Otherwise Grace has won. Hiring Amelia was a good decision. It's a good thing. Trust me, it is.' She nodded, inviting him to agree.

Leo trusted her judgement, and saw the logic in what she was saying. It didn't make it any easier though, knowing she was right. Instinct still made him want to follow the new nanny and always be conscious of where she was.

'Okay, you win,' he sighed. 'But I'll keep my business in town as brief as possible. I'll be back before the light goes.'

Mora smiled. 'That's better. Now, can you speed up, please? That mountain bus won't wait.'

* * *

Leo returned home tired and mud-streaked. He had left Lucio with his parents, who had begged to keep him overnight, and gone to work. He'd ended up hauling boxes of produce along with his men to get it done faster. The shipment was ready and the deadline met. Now he craved a long drink and a meal. The rainy season had begun with a vengeance. It had hindered the work and made it harder than it needed to be.

He found himself looking forward to dinner. Mora Sorrento was away and Lucio was safe with his grandparents, so it would just be him and Amelia.

Now why did that please him? Because he'd get more answers out of her, he decided. He'd get to know her, whether she liked it or not. Call it a security check. *Call it pleasure.*

He drove the jeep into the parking space under the loggia and stood for a moment once he'd got out, listening for her.

Feeling more relaxed, he headed for the door of the house and pushed it open, then stood still. It was quiet. He guessed the maids were finished for the day; they cleaned from morning till mid-afternoon. It was now about three o'clock. But where was Amelia?

He called out, his voice reverberating on the wooden panelling. The Spanish tiles glinted in the sun. There was a scent of wood polish, and a pervading silence. In an instant he knew she was gone.

He leapt up the stairs two, three at a time, flung open the bedroom doors, and looked in the nursery. No sign of her. Annoyance and fear mingled in his blood. He forced himself to be calm and tried to think clearly. Frustrated, he retraced his steps to the nursery. A book lay open on the floor. He picked it up. It was a story about a monkey wearing a red hat. It clicked in his memory. The chattering monkey; Amelia's shock at its boldness. Her reaction when he had suggested she shouldn't venture outside alone. She hadn't liked it one bit.

Had Amelia deliberately gone outside to provoke him? Leo paced furiously. His face darkened. He threw the book down. The spine broke with the force of his throw. The pages lay flat and forlorn.

Think. Think, Leo. Where had she gone? She could be anywhere. He snapped his fingers. The waterfall, where he had enjoyed many picnics and outings with Grace before she had left, while she had still pretended to be a loving wife. It lay at the end of the winding path that led from Grenville into the thick forest.

He wasted no time but set off immediately, dreading what he'd find. Had she vanished into the jungle; strayed from the path? His jaw tightened painfully as his thoughts of Amelia shifted from fury to worry. She was in some kind of trouble. His gut told him something was wrong. No one in their right mind would go out into the jungle in this kind of weather.

The rain was easing, but the water poured off the shiny leaves onto his skin as he strode into the damp, warm forest. The path was strewn with debris. Eventually it faded into a faint flattened line that was hard to make out.

Leo knew the forest well; even without the path he'd find the waterfall. God alone knew what it would look like after the storm. He broke through the vegetation and climbed over fallen logs. All the way, his heart pounding, he said her name. It was like a shadow that wouldn't go. What was he going to find?

And then he was there: the waterfall gushing down the rock face; the pool, swollen with the rains, seeping over the land. His gaze scanned the scene. Dammit, where was she? Then he heard a faint cry.

Leo's heart stopped. Amelia lay motionless. She was covered in mud, so he hadn't seen her at first. Now that he knew she was safe, a mixture of emotions churned in him: relief that she was there; fear that she was hurt; and suspicion, too. She wasn't off the hook yet. She was going to explain to him exactly why she had defied his orders. Until she woke up, he didn't know what to think.

He hunkered down and moved his ear carefully near her mouth. Thank God — she was alive. Her warm, faint breath tickled his earlobe.

'Can you hear me, Amelia?' he said, lifting her so that he cradled her body in his arms. Her wet hair gave off the scent of violets, reminiscent of the English countryside so far from his home. He lowered his mouth to the top of her head and kissed her; why, he didn't know. The touch of her soft hair feathered his lips. 'Wake up,' he whispered.

Her eyelids flickered, then opened. She was dazed. When she managed to focus, she frowned as if she didn't recognise him. Then her eyes widened and she gave him the sweetest smile. It turned his insides to liquid and tightened his groin — inappropriately, given the circumstances.

'You saved me,' she breathed. 'I prayed you'd find me.'

'Lucky for you that I did,' he replied harshly.

Her grey eyes were sad. 'I'm sorry,' she whispered. 'So sorry. I shouldn't have . . . ' She winced and cried out as he shifted her in his arms.

'What is it?' he asked swiftly, concerned.

'My ribs,' she said through whitened lips. 'Very painful.' She slumped forward and he caught her.

Her ribs were agony, but her heart was singing. Leo had found her. Relief washed over her. She was okay. She allowed herself to stop thinking about how she had to be brave; instead, she wallowed in the sensation of being in Leo's strong arms. She felt his body warmth seep into her, and the power of his muscles as he cradled her. He smelt of spice and damp cotton and masculinity. She wanted to burrow into his embrace and stay there.

She had dreamed he'd kissed her. It had seemed so real, the gentle pressure of his lips on her hair. A tender gesture. It had to be a dream. She hadn't seen a tender side to him — not for her, in any case. All his tenderness was for his child. There was no room for anyone else.

Amelia's mind was fuzzy. There was a terrible pain in her side. It made her gasp when she took a breath. So she was very annoyed when Leo forced her to stand. She cried out and punched his chest. Her fist landed on him like a feather.

Through a fog of discomfort, she

heard his voice, alternately bullying and gentling, for what felt like hours. Her legs were leaden, her head heavy. And always, there was Leo.

6

Amelia's ribs were bruised but not broken. Leo's fingers had probed and prodded. In turn, Amelia had gasped and bitten down on her lip. Finally, he'd pronounced she'd survive.

'Can you manage in the shower by yourself?' came his voice, clipped and unfriendly. An image of Leo helping her made her face heat up.

'Yes, thank you.' She risked a glance at him and wished she hadn't. His face was stony. The tension was tangible. He was furious with her, and Amelia didn't blame him. She was furious with herself.

The hot shower stung her skin and washed away the mud. If only it could wash away the events of the day so easily. If she hadn't decided to go for a picnic . . . to challenge him . . . What if the flash flood had swept her away? She squeezed her eyes shut. Whatever Leo had to say to her, it couldn't be worse than her own imaginings.

She went downstairs gingerly. Her ribcage was tender, but the pain was subsiding. She'd been lucky to escape with a few bruises. Leo was waiting for her in the dining room.

'Where's Lucio?' she asked.

'At my parents' house,' he said.

'Thank goodness. I wondered who you would have left him with, to come and find me.'

Leo let out a long breath and pressed his lips together. 'I would have left him with one of the maids in her house. There would have been no alternative.'

She felt even worse. Leo would hate to leave his son in another person's care. He didn't appear to trust anyone with the baby. His tone was forbidding, his face dark. She couldn't tell what he was thinking. He paced for a moment, then abruptly sat and motioned to her to take a seat. 'You must eat,' he told her.

There was a light meal laid before them: a platter of cold meats, salad, a wheat loaf, and grilled plantain. Amelia had no appetite, but Leo put a plate of food in front of her. There was a lump in her throat. No way could she swallow food. Instead, she caught Leo's gaze and almost flinched at his expression. The she found a reserve of courage from somewhere and managed to speak. 'I'm so sorry. I shouldn't have gone out. I shouldn't have — '

'Done the opposite of what I asked you to do,' Leo cut in sharply. His hands clenched as if he would strike the table. She saw him make a deliberate effort to stop. His fingers uncurled and he dropped his hands out of sight.

Amelia felt her own anger rise. Okay, she'd made an error in judgement. But she hadn't committed a crime! She jumped up angrily and winced as her ribs complained painfully. 'It was a picnic,' she said. 'That's all.'

His amber eyes sought hers. For a long moment they stared at each other.

It was as if he wanted to reach into her soul for answers. Then he looked away. There was a long silence. Just as Amelia was about to break it, Leo spoke.

'It wasn't just a picnic. Be honest. You weren't pleased to be told not to leave the compound on your own. So you decided to show me that you were boss. Am I right?'

She flushed. It was an uncomfortable truth. He could read her too well, and clearly it showed on her face.

'Ahh, Miss Knight's aversion to being controlled,' he sneered. 'So this is what it's about. Not about anyone else, but about flouting my authority. I say don't go beyond the house and grounds. And *you* say, 'I'll do what I like.' Yes?'

He had never sounded more foreign than at that moment. The island accent was strong and mocking. His words rang in her ears. There was more than an element of truth in them, and she didn't like hearing it.

Amelia's legs were weak. She sat

down. Although the evening was warm, her fingertips were icy. She rubbed them together distractedly. But nothing could distract her from the truth that Leo deserved to hear.

'You were right that I wanted to flout your authority. I knew you didn't want me to go outside the walls by myself. But really, what gives you the right to tell me where I can and cannot go?' Her voice had risen and she stopped abruptly, pulling a piece of bread from the loaf. It broke into crumbs under her fingers as she spoke again. 'The house was starting to feel like a prison,' she said, trying to make him understand. 'It reminded me of William's house in London.'

'In what way? You're free to come and go here at Grenville. No one's keeping you prisoner, despite what you might think.' His puzzled frown lit upon her face.

'I know that. But it felt restrictive when you warned me off going outside. Plus, I wanted to prove to you that I can cope with the island,' she admitted.

'Was life with your father restrictive?'

'That's an understatement.' She forced a bitter laugh. 'He told me what to wear; he decided what meals we'd eat; he'd only allow certain friends to visit at the house.' Never mind how he managed to deal with any man who had the courage to try to date her. 'The final straw was when he demanded I give up my job and work in the bank. I knew if I did that, I'd have absolutely no freedom at all.'

'But you did give up your job. You fled here.'

Amelia shook her head. 'I didn't give up my job in London. I was let go.'

'Let go? What did you do?'

'Nothing,' she said sadly. 'I did nothing wrong at all. William told my employers lies about me. When that didn't work, he put pressure on them to fire me. They felt guilty about it, but they buckled under his blackmail. I was let go, but at least they wrote me a good reference; otherwise Mora wouldn't have considered me for this job. William didn't know I got a reference; he thought he'd won and that I'd come crawling back to him and work in his business under his thumb.'

'But you didn't,' Leo said. 'You found this job instead.' He paused. 'Except I wouldn't let you have it when you got here. You didn't have many options left, Amelia. Why didn't you tell me?'

'How could I tell you? Would you have believed me?'

'No, probably not,' he admitted. He stood now, staring grimly at her across the width of table. 'How could I? You didn't tell me who you are until I forced you to. You wouldn't explain why you came here. So secretive, Amelia Knight.'

'If you distrusted me so much, why did you leave me alone here today?' she flung at him.

He shook his head. 'I shouldn't have. I blame myself for what happened today.'

'That's ridiculous. It was a mistake,

but it was *my* mistake. You are not in control of my actions. I am.' Now the table was no longer between them as Amelia stalked angrily round to his side of it. 'If you really distrust me, then I'll go upstairs and pack right away and leave tonight.' Her face was tilted up to his, and her eyes shone with a mixture of anger and hurt.

A pulse leapt in Leo's taut jaw and his brows were a black slash as he faced her. Battling emotions crossed his face. She was so close to him. With a groan, he closed the small distance and kissed her hard. His hands pressed against the back of her head while he did so.

Almost instantly, his mouth softened over hers and Amelia's lips parted. Her heart was thudding. Her body tingled with his touch and she wanted more. Her tongue slid over his and he pulled her closer. She felt his hardness. Her insides were liquid with need. Then he pushed her from him and steadied her. It was like being torn from where she *had* to be. In his embrace she'd felt for a moment completely in the right place in the world.

They were both breathing heavily. Amelia's chest rose and fell in agitation. Leo's dark golden eyes flashed in something like longing, or despair.

'I apologise,' he muttered. 'I don't know what I was thinking, doing that.'

'Let's forget it,' she agreed, knowing it was impossible for her to do so. The taste of him lingered on her lips and tongue. A sweetness like honey ran along her veins. She longed to kiss him again — which was wrong, all wrong. She was here to work for Leo Grenville, not to seduce him or be seduced by him. A thrill rippled through her and she tried to ignore it. She was still angry with him.

And he was still annoyed with her, too. Otherwise, why was he pacing so? Then he looked up and she saw turmoil on his face. His next words were not what she expected.

'I failed them both.'

'What do you mean? Who did you fail?'

'My son and my wife.' He shook his head impatiently. 'I should never have brought Grace here. She hated the island, the climate, the food. I should have seen the signs. I should've known she'd leave. When she went . . . I had no idea how to look after a small baby. So I hired a nanny. I shut myself away to lick my wounds. I was selfish, thinking only about my own heart-break. Meanwhile, the woman I had employed to look after my son was neglecting him just as much as his mother had done. But it took me far too long to see it. It's made it difficult for me to leave Lucio with someone else.'

Amelia's heart went out to him. Despite his grim expression, she wanted to run to him, curl her arms around him and comfort him.

'Grace didn't want children. The pregnancy was unplanned, but I thought that when she had the baby she'd fall in love with him immediately.' His mouth twisted. 'How wrong I was. She was neglectful and careless with him. She made it clear that she'd rather shop and party than look after a baby. Grace was prone to whims and enthusiasms that never lasted. Lucio was one of them, a baby sometimes smothered in love by his mother and then the next day ignored. She was never happy here. The climate didn't suit her and neither did the culture, the isolation of small-island life. We're learning to live without her.' He gave a humourless laugh.

Amelia's fingers pressed on the table. She didn't speak; she needed to hear the rest of what Leo had to say.

'Of course she'll never get him back. When she left us, she gave up her rights to my son.' His voice hardened.

Amelia shivered. The image of the panther rose like smoke in her mind. She could easily see Leo telling his ex-wife that. There was a core of steel to him. He was not a man to cross lightly.

He sat, too, and pushed the plates of food across to her. 'Eat,' he said. 'You must be hungry.'

She took a few slices of the meat and a portion of salad to be polite. But when she began to eat, she realised she was starving. Across from her, Leo concentrated on his own plate. For a short while they ate in silence. But Amelia's head was full of their conversation — and that kiss. It had come out of nowhere.

Not true, she argued. What *was* true was that their mutual attraction had exploded. Even if they shouldn't have kissed, it heated her blood to know that Leo found her desirable, though he'd made it clear it was a mistake. Her spirits swooped. Had she really expected it to be otherwise? She was here to work for him, and besides, there were too many other reasons for her not to get involved. His natural masterfulness. The shadow of William still in the background of her thoughts. The complication of getting involved with her employer when she needed this job so badly.

'You think you proved to me you can survive here on the island?' Leo said suddenly, a slight smile tugging at his mouth. 'You were camouflaged with mud, like a half-drowned creature, when I found you.'

'Well, I . . . ' she began indignantly, then had to laugh.

Leo laughed too, a warm, deep sound that mingled with hers. It felt suddenly good, as if the tense atmosphere had vaporised. 'I'm sorry,' he said. 'I shouldn't have said that. You did well out there.'

'But I shouldn't have been there in the first place,' she said. Why did his warm expression make her stomach do little flips?

He shrugged. 'Maybe next time we'll go together.'

'Would you like that?' she spoke without thinking. Then she focused on her empty plate and made a show of tidying the cutlery, then pouring drinks

119

from the bottle of wine Leo had produced.

'Yes, I would,' he said softly.

The bottle clinked the rim of the wine glass clumsily and he reached and took it from her. His fingers touched hers ever so briefly, but the ripple of sensation ran the length of her arm like a shockwave. She curled her fingers in so that her nails bit into her palms. Reality check. That was better. Bring the conversation back into sharp focus. 'I'm not going to promise not to go outside again.'

'I could make you promise.'

She stiffened, a prickle of resentment starting in her middle. Then she saw the slow smile teasing his lips.

Leo was enjoying baiting her. He liked to see her serious grey eyes widen as he teased. She was too earnest. He wanted to see her smile; to watch those luscious full lips widen and part. It had been wrong to kiss her; a spontaneous reflex he couldn't contain. He remembered the pressure of her soft mouth on his. How sweet she tasted. The tender fragility of her skull as he cradled her head. It must not happen again — but he was finding it hard to think why.

He poured more wine. The house was quiet. He was all too aware that Mora was away overnight and that his son was safely asleep at his parents' home, miles away. It was just him and Amelia. His mind battled with his body and won. He knew all the reasons why it was wrong to be attracted to her. He would not have a fling with someone in his employ. It was taking advantage of his position as her employer. And a longer relationship? It was impossible. Grace had torn out his heart when she left. He would never go through that again.

He was impressed with Amelia almost against his will. She might be small and slender, but she hadn't given up when faced with danger. She had so nearly made it to safety on the ledge. And she had fought fiercely for her job the day he'd met her and dismissed her so readily. Now he understood her tenacity. He admired it.

There was more to Miss Amelia Knight than met the eye. She was no startling beauty, just a slim girl with fair hair and big grey eyes. But he was beginning to see her inner qualities shine through, and he couldn't deny that he found her extremely attractive. Why, he'd no idea. Was it the scattering of freckles across her cheeks that disallowed any sophistication? Her slim waist and surprisingly curvy body? Or, more likely, the fact that she stood up to him, and the way her face showed her feelings so refreshingly?

The fact was, since the events of the day, he trusted her with his son. But he didn't trust his own emotions when she was around.

The telephone rang, and Leo left the room to answer it. Amelia heard his deep voice rising in argument; then there was silence before he spoke more steadily. She sat up and gasped. Her ribs were tender once more, as the painkillers had worn off. It had been a rollercoaster of a day; but funnily, she felt closer to Leo now that she knew about Grace. A lick of jealousy flickered in her chest. Did Leo still love his wife? Was that why the story was still painful for him to tell? Was that why he apologised for their kiss?

She gave herself a mental shake. Of course the kiss was wrong. She didn't want that complication either — did she?

Leo came back, looking annoyed. 'My parents have invited us to lunch on Saturday.'

'You and Lucio,' Amelia corrected. 'Not me, surely?'

He shrugged impatiently. 'Of course you must come as well. Lucio will need his nanny when he gets tired from all the attentions of his grandmother and aunties and uncles.'

The nanny. Why did it sting to hear him dismiss her that way? It was stupid of her. Of course she would be invited along to look after the child. That was why she was here, after all.

'You don't sound too pleased with the invitation,' she said hesitantly. 'If you don't want to go, why didn't you make your excuses?' He was known as a recluse. Mora had explained to her that Leo didn't go visiting.

'You've clearly never met my mother.' He sighed, and in that moment looked much younger. 'My brother is home from New York for a holiday, and she insists on my coming to lunch and bringing you to be introduced to the Grenville family.'

7

Amelia went downstairs with a thumping headache. It might have been due to the humidity, or it could be the fact that they were due at the Grenville family house for lunch. She was nervous, which was stupid. They weren't going to pay attention to her. She was there to be the nanny, nothing more. So really, did it matter what kind of an impression she made?

But she felt that it did matter. Why, she wasn't able to say. Maybe she didn't want to let Leo down. Was that it? No, that was ridiculous. She didn't care about his opinion of her. She was good at her job, and that was all that was required.

She went into the cool interior of the living room. Mora and Lucio had gone out to town. She was glad to see that Leo was letting his son have a little more freedom. It was done cautiously, but he was getting there. Mora seemed pleased with this too. So now Amelia was at a loose end until they came back.

Idly she rearranged the cushions and tidied the coffee table surface. She decided she'd take a walk around the grounds, then prepare dinner as a surprise for Mora. She turned to go out and smacked straight into Leo.

'Oh.' Her hands flattened on his hard chest. They thrummed with sensation and she snatched them back. 'What are you doing, sneaking up on me like that?' she snapped, shaken by his nearness.

'Hey,' he said softly, putting his hands up in mock surrender, 'I said your name twice. Your head's in the clouds. You didn't hear me at all.'

'Sorry,' Amelia said, stepping back and trying for composure. 'I was deciding what to do this morning. I'm a bit lost without Lucio.'

Leo's mouth dipped in a wry grin. 'Me too.'

'But it's good you let him go to the market with Mora,' Amelia said quickly.

'You think I'm making progress?' Leo smiled. His gaze was warm and teasing.

'I do,' she said primly, while her body raged. He was so close. She saw the tiny lines around his mouth; the crinkles at his eyes; the way his thick black hair curled ever so slightly over his collar.

'He'll be fine,' Leo said. It was said firmly, as if he were speaking to himself, but his eyes sought hers.

'Yes, he will be fine.' Suddenly she couldn't look away.

A peal of parrot calls broke the odd silence that stretched between them. Leo reached for a box on the floor beside him and gave it to her.

'What's this?' she asked.

'You could open it and find out. There's nothing in it that bites or flies, I promise.'

'Hmmm. In this place, can I be sure of that?' She wrinkled her nose, remembering the beetle. With mounting curiosity, she slit the tape holding the cardboard lid on and opened the box. Inside, nestled in pale green tissue paper, was a pair of the most gorgeous sandals she'd seen. They were leaf-green with gold trim and slim heels.

'They're beautiful,' she breathed, looking up at him. 'Did you get these for me?'

'They wouldn't suit me.'

'How did you know what size to get?' *Ever practical. Way to go, Amelia. An attractive man buys you the most fantastic pair of shoes, and that's all you can say?*

'I got yours out of the rubbish,' Leo said with a shrug.

'But . . . why would you do this for me?' She put the box down on the coffee table.

'You don't like them?'

'Of course I like them. They're wonderful. But why did you get them?'

'I remember you told me your sandals made you feel good,' he said softly. 'You bought them the day you left your father's house. I think they gave you courage and hope for your new life. I want you to feel like that when you wear these.'

Sunlight streamed into the room. Amelia saw flecks of pure gold in his irises. For a moment it all seemed possible, but then reality crashed in. He wasn't an attractive man buying her shoes — he was her boss. And they looked really expensive.

'I can't accept them.' She shook her head reluctantly.

'Why not?' He looked surprised.

'Leo . . . I work for you. That's why. It'd be inappropriate for me to accept such a gift.' Now she sounded like a pompous idiot. Great. What she really meant was that it was far too intimate.

'Inappropriate? No, Amelia, it's simply practical. Your own sandals were destroyed the day you arrived at my house. We're visiting my parents today, and I'd like you to be well turned out. So . . . ' He shrugged carelessly. 'So you will wear the sandals — if you wish.'

'I thought . . . ' She didn't know what to say. *I thought it was a man-to-woman sort of gift*. Her toes curled in embarrassment. She'd totally misread his intentions. He just wanted her to look presentable when she met his parents as his employee, nanny to his son. It would look bad for him if the nanny was a complete scruff. Yet disappointment sank her heart. It was a practical present. There was nothing of Leo himself in it. Which was how it should be, she told herself.

He was still waiting for a response. His face gave nothing away about what he was thinking. She forced a smile. 'Thank you. It was good of you to get them. I'll wear them today.'

'Excellent. We'll leave at midday. I'll see you then.' His manner was brisk and to the point.

When he'd gone, Amelia picked up the sandals and stroked the soft leather. He was right; she had no suitable shoes to wear for the family lunch invitation, so he had provided a solution. She went back upstairs to lay them on her bed. Then it struck her that the colour of the sandals perfectly complemented that of her green summer dress. She'd worn it several times since she'd arrived on the island. She stopped in the middle of taking it off its hanger from the wardrobe. Was it coincidence, or had Leo chosen the sandals to match her dress?

★　★　★

What a fool he was! He shouldn't have bought the damned shoes for her. Leo swore under his breath as he buttoned his fresh shirt at the mirror. His neck was uncomfortable with the stiff collar. With a snarl, he tore the shirt off and flung it away. To hell with formality. He'd wear a plain day-shirt and no tie. His parents liked their sons to dress up for family occasions, but today he didn't care.

He'd wanted . . . what, exactly? Amelia's gratitude? For those big grey eyes to light up for him? He knew how much her own sandals had meant to her. They were a symbol of her freedom. He'd wanted to recreate that, to show her that what she was striving for was possible and that he admired her for it. That was all.

Except that somehow he'd messed up with the gift. In trying to explain, he'd given it too much value — that was it. And so she'd refused to accept them. Then he'd gone wrong again by pretending it meant nothing; was just a practical replacement of her shoes. He groaned. She'd looked as if he'd slapped her across the face. He couldn't figure any of it out.

He selected a pair of charcoal-grey trousers and a casual jacket, then glanced at his watch. Five to midday. It was time to go.

★ ★ ★

Grenville family get-togethers were inevitably busy and noisy, and today was no exception. Leo's parents lived in a sprawling white stucco ranch house on the west coast of Trinita. Bougainvillea trees splashed vivid crimson and purple colour in the courtyard, and lemon trees hung heavy with early fruit, their citrus scent pervading the warm afternoon air.

The patio was set with a variety of chairs and tables laden with different dishes and drinks. Leo's father, Jose, stooped over the huge barbecue, which curled with grey smoke, while Leo's younger brother, Joe, gave cooking directions and waved a long skewer about dangerously.

Instinctively, Leo cast around for Amelia. His family were all good, warm-hearted people, but en masse they could be daunting. He'd been inside, getting grilled by his mother over his health and working too hard. Escaping on the pretext of helping Jose and Joe, he stopped and scanned.

He caught a flash of green. She was wearing the summer dress he liked, the one that he'd carefully chosen the sandals to go with. He cast an appreciative long glance down her slim legs and ankles to the damned footwear. Yes, they suited her, as did the dress, which clung in all the right places.

There was a nudge at his side. Daniel stood beside him. 'Hey, big brother. How're you? More to the point, who's that?' There was a gleam in his eyes as he indicated where Amelia stood talking to Leo's two sisters-in-law.

'That, little brother, is Lucio's new nanny.' Leo went for a mild voice. Always best with Daniel, who was an inveterate wind-up merchant.

'If I wasn't a married man . . . ' Daniel winked wickedly. 'I can see why you chose her. Nice and easy on the eye.'

'I didn't choose her.' Leo's voice heated up. 'And you should watch your mouth and be respectful. She's good at her job.'

'I see,' Daniel said with a slow smile.

'It's like that, is it?'

'It's not like anything,' Leo said stiffly. 'Why don't you go help Papi with the barbecue?'

Daniel clapped him hard on the back. 'I'm kidding with you. Besides, it's not me, it's Mama you need to worry about. She loves playing match-maker, as you know. It worked out good for me and Wendy.'

'As I remember, you didn't need much encouragement to chase her,' Leo said drily.

Daniel laughed. 'Very true. I fell in love with Wendy like falling off a cliff. I had to beg her to put my ring on her finger.'

'That's because she knows she's too good for you.' Brothers jibing as usual. It was easy to fall back into the old sibling behaviour, familiar and loving. He'd stayed away from them too long.

As if catching his thoughts, Daniel said, 'Mama misses you. Papi too. You should visit more often. Let the past go, Leo. It shouldn't take Joe visiting from the States to get you over here. Mama deserves to see you, and she misses Lucio.'

Daniel left him and went over to speak to Joe. Leo watched him go. It had worked out well for Daniel. He'd married Wendy and now had two children, Lara and Kenny, who were growing up healthy and fast. He tried not to feel a twinge of envy and failed.

He'd go and find out if Amelia was okay. He took a step forward and stopped. She was chatting and laughing with Wendy and Joe's wife, Neeva, and had Lucio in her arms. She leant down and stroked his face. Her expression was so tender and loving that Leo forgot to breathe.

'Give him to me, I'll take him to his nana.' He sounded stern, and forced his voice to be calm. The three young women were staring at him.

Leo tried again with a smile. 'She wants to see her *bebe*.'

Amelia smiled uncertainly and passed Lucio to him.

'We were telling Amelia the story of your teenage camping trip,' Neeva said brightly into the awkward pause.

Leo was grateful to her; Neeva was always the one to smooth over situations. She was a kind, gentle person. Joe was a lucky guy.

'Not that old tale again.' He was relieved to hear he sounded normal.

Amelia was laughing as Wendy continued the story of the brothers' disastrous camp-out in the jungle. Her hair shone in the strong sunshine, and her face was tanned and healthy. She looked gorgeous — and as if she belonged. His jaw tightened. Seeing her with Lucio . . . with his family . . .

'Excuse me,' he muttered and strode back to the house with his child, knowing that three puzzled faces were watching him go.

Amelia couldn't make him out. The evening they were alone in the house, she'd felt close to understanding him; felt he'd softened towards her, too. Now it was like the shutters had slammed down. What had she done? She wracked her brain and came up with nothing. She was enjoying talking to Neeva and Wendy. She was tending to Lucio, although Sancia, Leo's mother, had already told her not to worry about that, as Wendy's kids loved to keep an eye on him. Amelia must relax and enjoy being a guest, Sancia had said firmly.

Neeva lifted her shoulders. 'Before you ask, I don't know what he's about either. Probably got into an argument with Joe.'

'Or Daniel,' Wendy said with a grin.

'Don't they get along?' Amelia asked.

'Oh yes, they all get on,' Wendy said. 'But you know how brothers and sisters are.'

No, she didn't. She'd have loved a sister to talk to. It might've made her life a lot easier; taken William's focus off her.

'Do you come from a big family?' Wendy was asking.

'No.' She really didn't want to go into

it, but softened her answer with a smile. Wendy took the hint and didn't say more.

Neeva said warmly, 'Now you've been introduced to the Grenville clan, you've got a ready-made family.'

How would that feel, to be a part of this wonderful, loving bunch of people? Amelia had liked them all immediately. Leo's father was a tall, quiet man, but she noticed that they all stopped to listen when he spoke. There was respect and love there. Leo's brothers were amusing and fun. They were also drop-dead gorgeous, like him. All three had the same dark good looks. And Daniel and Joe were clearly besotted with their pretty wives. Amelia felt at once encircled by the family's friendliness and excluded because she wasn't one of them.

She compared the atmosphere with that of her own home and shivered. It made her life with William seem even worse. She hadn't truly known what she was missing in her family. There was a catch in her throat. 'Sorry, I'll be back in a minute,' she said, needing a moment to recover her poise. The house looked like the best bet. There was no sign of Leo, and she hoped not to bump into him.

Instead she met Sancia. Leo's mother was taking a tray of warmed rolls from the vast oven. Her eyes brightened at the sight of Amelia. She took off her apron and laid it down.

'Amelia, just the person I need. Can you help me gather some flowers from the side garden for the centrepiece?'

'What about the rolls? Shouldn't I take those out for you?'

Sancia waved her arms airily. 'No, no, I told Leo to take them. He's about somewhere. Come along — you take the basket, I take the scissors.' She swept Amelia along with her and out of a side door. They entered a peaceful walled garden full of blossoming shrubs and plants. Beyond, they could hear the chatter and smell the barbecue.

'We won't be long,' Sancia promised.

'Just a few bunches of my *bella* flowers.'

Leo's mother was like a small, determined whirlwind. She had the same black thick hair as her three sons, but her eyes were dark too and flashed when she spoke vigorously. Amelia began to see where Leo got his strength and steely character from.

'Are you happy at the estate?' Sancia asked, pulling at a yellow flower and snipping its stem expertly. She handed it to Amelia.

'I haven't been there long, but yes, I'm happy.'

'It's a wonderful place. Jose and I were also very happy there.'

'I didn't realise you lived there. When did you move here?' Amelia asked.

'Ah, well.' Sancia sighed. She took a moment to cut some stems and give them to Amelia before going on. 'It must be four years ago. The Grenville estate has been in the family for generations. My husband and I worked it until he got ill. At first I didn't notice he was slowing down, but then it finally got to be too much for him. The doctor told him he must give up working or his heart would do so.' She put down the scissors and looked at Amelia. 'Leo was in London. He was on business there, and he had met Grace. I told him that he had to come home; had to come and help his papi. That it was his duty as the eldest son. And so he came home and brought Grace with him. They got married, and Leo began to run the estate. Jose and I bought this house to retire to.'

She picked up the scissors and cut some waxy red flowers. Amelia stored them in her almost-full basket. Her mind was full of imagining Leo and his new bride returning to the island after the cosmopolitan appeal of London. How had Grace felt? Had it been the return to Trinita that had soured their relationship?

'He's an honourable man,' Sancia said, 'my son.' She pushed a stray hair from her forehead and stood up. 'He'll do what's right. Always. But I blame myself for what happened with Grace. I encouraged him to marry her. She was beautiful and mannered, and seemed so right for him. But she hurt him badly.' Her dark eyes glanced at Amelia. 'He's very proud, you know. He doesn't find it easy to give way to others. But he has a good heart.'

'Mrs Grenville . . . ' Amelia paused. 'I don't know why you're telling me this.'

'Sancia. Call me Sancia.'

'Sancia . . . I'm here to work. Leo is . . . ' *Leo is what? You're going to tell his mother that he's kind, and good, and so damned attractive you can't stop thinking about him?* She shut her mouth.

Sancia laughed. 'Leo is Leo. And I'm his mother. I can see into his soul. And I see that he likes you. He likes you very much. And that can be a good thing. Or it can go bad. You see what I'm saying?'

'Not really.' Leo liked her? Amelia's heart danced.

'You seem like a lovely young woman. I have to hope that you're not like Grace.'

'I'm only here to work,' Amelia said politely but firmly. 'Please believe me. I'm fully absorbed with looking after Lucio, and that's quite sufficient for me.'

The mention of Sancia's grandson diverted her, and she shot several questions at Amelia about Lucio's health and energy and intelligence. It was obvious that to his grandmother he was the most talented boy ever — except of course for Kenny, who was just like his sister Lara.

Relieved that the conversation had turned away from Leo, Amelia let the older woman talk, and answered when she had to. So Leo hadn't wanted to run the Grenville estate; he'd been forced back to Trinita by his father's ill health. How had Grace felt, having to follow him here? Once she'd got pregnant, had she felt trapped?

Amelia tried to feel empathy with Grace and failed. If it had been her, she'd have felt blessed to join such a lovely family; to have a child. *With Leo.*

It popped into her head. She loved children and did want to have some of her own one day. But she'd never visualised who the father might be. It was madness triggered, she decided, by Sancia Grenville's blatant matchmaking.

Sancia gestured her through now that they had enough flowers, and Amelia was suddenly eager to get to the barbecue. Surely Leo was there, helping his brothers and his father. She wanted a chance to thank him properly for her sandals. It had all gone wrong earlier. She wanted to make it up to him.

8

The family were all seated at the long tables, passing food round, as Amelia joined them. She slipped into the empty chair next to Leo. Sancia smiled at her. She guessed that particular chair had been left for her on purpose. She wasn't sure whether to feel exasperated by Leo's mother or to find the whole thing amusing. One glance at Leo, however, and she knew how he felt. He was politely replying to Wendy about a question she'd asked, but he was reserved. She sensed his muscle tension, an awareness of him that she had that was uncanny. What she didn't know was why he was tense. What had gone wrong?

'Have you settled in at the Grenville estate, Amelia?' Daniel asked, looking at both Leo and Amelia with a sly grin. 'Is Lucio being a good baby for Nanny?'

'Well of course she's settled. How could she fail to be, with such a beautiful *bebe* to look after?' Sancia said with a satisfied smile at her sons. 'As an excellent nanny, she knows how to take care of Lucio. Leo is satisfied. Am I right?' She turned to Leo and waited for his answer.

'You're right,' he said. There was a brief softening in his amber eyes as he acknowledged Amelia. He seemed to think better of it, and then the cool, polite and reserved Leo was back fast.

Amelia was bewildered. As the conversation moved on to other topics, she tried to think if she'd done anything to make him act that way, but couldn't come up with anything. Perhaps family get-togethers stressed him out. But whatever the cause, she decided to ignore his bad mood. It was a beautiful day; the food and company were good. She'd enjoy it. Forget Leo.

As if. It wasn't possible, when he was sitting right next to her. His arm brushed hers and tingles rushed across her skin. She was too conscious of his long, muscled thighs as he stretched his legs out under the table. It was time to admit it to herself: she had *never* been this attracted to any man. Ever.

The food was eaten and everyone was shaking their heads at third helpings, seconds having been success-fully distributed by Sancia. She was a perfect hostess, making sure they all had heaped plates and full glasses. Now she was met by groans when she offered more.

'Leo, I have a good idea,' she said. 'Why don't you show Amelia your father's new project? I'm sure she'll be fascinated.'

'Great, I'll walk with you,' Daniel said lazily. He winked at Joe.

'No, no.' Sancia's hands windmilled at her second son. 'I need you to help carry in the dishes. Joe, you too. Wendy and Neeva will wash up, you two can dry.'

'I'll help too,' Amelia offered awk-wardly.

But Sancia turned her down and gave her son a black stare until he shifted in his seat.

'My mother isn't known for her subtlety,' Leo murmured in Amelia's ear. 'For an easy life, it's best to agree with her.'

He stood up and waited for Amelia to follow. The others had been herded to the kitchen by Sancia. Jose dozed in his chair. He was considerably older than his energetic wife, Amelia realised.

'Where are we going?' she asked as she followed Leo round the side of the house.

'My father has designed a carp pond. It was constructed a few weeks ago. I haven't seen it yet.'

She sped up to match his stride. It wasn't far to the new pond, which was more like a small lake. It was fringed by palm trees and large pampas grasses and was very peaceful.

'We must hide here for at least a half hour to give my mother satisfaction,' Leo said with dry humour. 'Then we can return for interrogation.'

'I like your mother,' Amelia said. 'Your whole family is lovely; they've been very welcoming.'

'Don't get to liking them too much. You won't see them often.'

She flinched at his tone. 'It's okay, Leo, you don't have to warn me off. I'm not trying to worm my way in. I do understand that my position as nanny is more like that of a servant than a guest. Your mother was simply being very kind to me today to treat me as a visitor. I won't expect that next time.' Her voice was stiff with hurt.

Leo winced and put his hand out, but let it drop before he touched her. He blew out a breath. He wasn't being fair to her. The image of Lucio in her arms steeled his heart. He had to make her understand why none of this could be permanent, despite wanting to kiss away the misery in her eyes; misery that he had caused. He stiffened his spine. It was necessary. Better to push her away now than create heartache for everyone later.

'I wanted to say . . . ' Amelia began.

But Leo cut over her. 'What I meant, about my family, was that there's no point in getting to know them. I didn't mean that you're not good enough to mix with us. For heaven's sake, that's ridiculous. We don't separate into master and servant like the olden days.' He shook his head impatiently. How could he get his point across? Firstly, by not looking at her face. His resolve must not falter. His deepening attraction to her could not be considered. If anything, it made it even more important that he tell her.

'What, then?' she cried. 'What have I done wrong? You're cross with me, I can tell. But I don't know why.'

His shoulders went down. 'I'm not cross with you. I'm cross with myself.'

'Why?' She sounded bewildered.

Leo didn't blame her. He wasn't making much sense. He paced the tiles and ran his fingers through his hair as if it would clear his brain. Images flashed in front of him: Lucio peaceful in her embrace; Amelia's tenderness with the child; the sweetness of her face as she spoke to him. He pressed his lips together and spoke tersely. 'You're very good with my son. You like him?'

'Yes, I'm very fond of him. Leo . . . what is this?'

'My first concern has to be Lucio. I don't want him to get too fond of you.'

'Why not? I hope very much that he does like me. Why shouldn't he like his nanny?'

'Because it'll break his heart when you leave.' He kicked pebbles from the tiles and saw the ripples as they vanished under the water's surface.

'I don't want to leave.' Amelia was stock still, a motionless figure shaded by the palms.

Leo clenched his fists. 'You don't want to leave just now. But one day, you will. I can't risk it. I can't have my boy's heart ripped out. He suffers from the empty space where his mother should be. There must be no more loss in his life. Do you understand what I'm saying?' *And no more loss in mine.*

Her slight figure moved. The skirt of the green dress that he liked so much rippled in the warm breeze. It slid across the shape of her legs, and he felt a jolt of pure *want*. He had to fight against it; battle the urges that hit his body like a sledgehammer.

'I haven't signed a contract yet. But I guess after the three-month trial, my contract will be a short one then.'

He nodded, relieved that her voice was even. She understood. 'So you see, it's for the best,' he said. He was glad this conversation was over. Though the thought of Amelia leaving Grenville made him feel strangely low.

'Is it? Isn't it cruel never to let Lucio get attached to other people?' Now her voice rose passionately. 'Is he only allowed to love you? Life isn't like that, Leo. It's ups and downs. People do come and go throughout our lives. He needs to learn to cope with that, like the rest of us. You're wrong. You're creating a cold environment for him to live in.'

'You . . . '

'No, you need to listen.' She stood close to him, her face tilted up. He saw every individual freckle across her cheeks; the way her eyelashes were brown, but black-tipped, as if dipped in ink; the stormy sea-colour of her gaze; the moistness of her lips as they parted to speak; a strand of fair hair curling at her temple. 'Grace has gone. It is awful, and she did a terrible, unforgivable thing in leaving. But does that give you the right to keep your son from ever forming loving relationships with other people? Does he have to suffer because you've suffered?'

'Are you saying that I'm a cold person?' Leo felt anything but as he stared at her. He could feel the heat radiating from her, she was so close.

The conversation had got out of hand. Amelia's nerves were humming like the strings of a violin. Their gazes were locked. Her breathing was erratic.

She had called him cold. But he was the opposite of cold. The panther was back, coiled and ready to spring. She knew if she touched him, his muscles would be hard like rock.

She had to apologise. She'd let her anger get in the way, and shouldn't have spoken about Grace. She had no idea how he felt about his ex-wife; whether or not he was still in love with her. Still, Leo was glaring down at her.

She opened her mouth to say sorry, and Leo's came down on hers with a muffled groan. His lips were hard and unforgiving until she moved into his embrace. They were like two halves of a mechanism slotting together, without thought or logic. Amelia kissed him back with fervent eagerness — tasting him, feeling the shape of his mouth and teeth with her tongue, letting his tongue invade her to taste and explore.

There was no room for words, for explanation. There could be no explanation. This was something she *needed*. It was clearly what Leo needed too. His body was all hard muscle as he pulled her in close. It made her blood boil, and her body ached painfully for more than his embrace. He stroked her hair and then her back. His fingers found the outer curves of her breasts, and the sensation drove her crazy.

Suddenly he stopped. The warmth of his mouth was gone; the aching touch of his hands vanished. His breath was ragged. He stood back and put a foot's breadth of space between them. Amelia's blood was still thundering in her veins. Her mouth felt bruised; her breasts were heavy with sensation. With a shaking hand, she smoothed back her ruffled hair and tidied it, then shifted her dress back to normal.

'That proves . . . ' Leo's voice cracked. He gave a cough and began again. 'That proves my point.'

'What point? The one about you being cold, or the one about me having to leave?'

'Perhaps we've got it out of our systems now,' Leo said with a dark frown, not answering her sarcastic question. 'You can't deny the attraction that's simmered between us since we met.'

It hadn't rid her system of it; it had stoked the embers into a bright and burning fire. She'd known how very attracted she was to Leo. After that kiss, their physical closeness, she burned for more. She risked a glance at him. He didn't look too happy. His brows were drawn together. A little muscle flickered in his jaw. He stared into the pond as if looking for answers.

Somehow she had to put this right. Leo had made it very clear that he didn't want attachments. She didn't want to lose her job. A brief affair might rupture all that. Yet, how could they avoid each other? How could they extinguish their desire? Was it better to have a short but intense fling? As Leo said, just get it out of their systems? She didn't know.

'What did you want to say to me?' Leo asked, surprising her out of her swirling thoughts.

'Pardon?'

'Earlier, before we . . . I interrupted you when you were going to tell me something.'

She thought back. It was like time had expanded. Before the kiss. After the kiss. Except it wasn't really a kiss; it was a whole experience of him — one she was desperate for more of. She remembered what she'd wanted to say. 'I was going to thank you properly for my sandals.'

His amber gaze flickered over her face. Her lower lip was still pulsating from the pressure of his kiss. A small smile lifted a corner of his mouth crookedly. She flushed.

'I don't mean like that,' she said, seeing the direction of his thoughts — a kiss to thank him.

'You're right,' Leo said. 'We gave in to this strange attraction once already. We don't have to go there again. Right?'

Amelia felt a peak of unreasonable irritation. *Strange* attraction? That implied he was puzzled about why he found her attractive. Maybe she ought to show him why. She pretended to stretch her shoulders back, letting her chest strain at her dress material. She had the satisfaction of seeing his adam's apple bob as he swallowed.

'Your sandals,' he said thickly. 'You don't need to thank me for them.'

She took pity on him and went back to her normal posture. 'No, I do. I wasn't very gracious earlier. It was a kind gift and I do appreciate them.' She threw him a sly look. 'They match the colour of my dress perfectly.'

'I had to hunt for a while to get the right shade,' he admitted.

'So, not quite a practical present then. Otherwise, beige leather would've done. Goes with everything.'

'That never occurred to me. I might've saved hours in the town. Shopping is not my favourite pastime.' Leo grimaced.

It touched her to think of him spending time getting the sandals for her. 'Why did you?'

'Like I said, your sandals were important to you — a symbol of what's possible. I want you to feel that courage and hope every day.'

There was a lump in her throat. 'I will. When I wear them, I'll feel strong.'

'You are strong. If your father saw you, he'd be proud of you.'

Amelia sighed. 'I wonder if that's true. I sometimes think he's probably glad to be rid of me, after all. It wasn't healthy for either of us in that house. I hope he finds happiness.' Though it was hard to imagine. William had been a harsh person all her life, with few friends.

'You said that people come and go in our lives; that we have to learn to cope. Are you talking about your mother?'

Amelia nodded. 'Yes. She died when I was ten. I missed her so much. I wanted to share my grief with William, but he kept me at a distance. With an adult perspective, I can see that in his own way he was grieving too. But as a child, it felt like he hated me. When he sent me to boarding school I closed in on myself for ages until I came to terms with losing her.'

'And him.'

'What?'

'You lost your father too. It was his choice to send you away, so in a way you lost both parents.'

'I never thought of it like that. But yes, you're right.'

'Poor Amelia.' He drew her close and she let him. It wasn't desire, simply comfort from one human being to another. She felt him press a kiss to her head. His arms were solid and warm around her. She wanted to curl up inside his embrace. A safe place. She savoured the moment, then pulled back.

'But I coped. That's the point, Leo. It's all part of living and loving. You can't shelter Lucio from all of that.'

But she wasn't just talking about the child. Leo was hiding from pain too, living a reclusive sort of life at the

Grenville estate, hardly even visiting his family. Grace must've hurt him badly. And he must've loved her so much for that to be the case.

'Did you want to come back to Trinita?' she asked him.

'What?'

'When your father was ill. Did you want to return?'

'I see my mother has been filling you in on my family history.'

'Did you blame them for what happened with Grace?' She held her breath.

He stared at the pond for so long she thought he'd forgotten her. Then, just as Amelia was about to make a move — walk away or speak to him, she wasn't sure which — he spoke.

'Sometimes I did. I believed . . . for a while . . . that if Grace and I had stayed in London, we would have been happy. But now I wonder . . . is that the basis of true love for someone — if you can only be happy together in one place? Is it real?'

He stared right at her. Amelia stared back. Did he expect an answer? Because she really didn't have one. No, that wasn't right. She knew what she believed. But she couldn't tell Leo that.

'I don't blame my parents. It was my duty to return to help them. I couldn't have lived with myself otherwise. I failed Grace, no one else.'

What about Grace? Amelia thought. Didn't she have to take some of the blame for the break-up of Leo's marriage? What kind of woman deserted her husband and tiny baby son just because she didn't like where they were living?

'We should go back now. They'll be wondering if we've drowned in the pond,' he said in an attempt at humour.

'So you're not going to talk about it,' she said, challenging him.

'No, I'm not. And what I said earlier still stands. You mustn't get too fond of Lucio. It can't last. I'm sorry, but it's for the best.'

He stalked away from her, round the

side of the house. Amelia stood there for a moment. The pond was peaceful, the palm fronds swaying in the slight breeze. She hadn't got through to him at all. Sancia was right. What had she said about Leo — ? He didn't find it easy to give way to others. Too right. He hadn't given way to Amelia at all. Her arguments had had no impact, not one little bit.

There was nothing for it but to go back to the patio and his family. When she got there, the party was breaking up. Daniel and Wendy and their kids were saying goodbye. Lucio was in Leo's arms, asleep. Sancia saw her and waved her over to join them. Leo turned now, too, and she saw the likeness of the father in the son. Two Grenville generations. And she didn't want to leave either of them.

9

Amelia's dart quivered pathetically on the wall beside the board. She was whiling away a wet afternoon while the baby slept soundly in the cot next to the wall. The air was full of warm moisture, even inside the house. The rainy season was at its peak. Amelia had seen the maids collecting frogs from the veranda walls and putting them back outside. Everywhere, it seemed, was damp and hot, and no one could get comfortable.

'Try, try again,' she said, gathering up the handful of darts. In fact, those words could sum up her entire life.

She threw another dart and shook her head when it missed the target and suckered to the wall. She made a face and stuck her tongue out.

'Need some help?' She spun round. Leo was watching her with a grin.

'No, I don't. I'm doing fine.' She saw his surprise at her reply. She couldn't help it. There was a large part of her that couldn't cope with someone else being in control, even Leo. Especially Leo. She'd seen him interact with Mora and Lucio and his estate staff. They all loved him, it was clear. He had a way of asking people to do things that wasn't demanding. But he usually got what he wanted — that was the wrinkle. That was what made her refuse his help.

'Doing fine?' he teased. 'I've been watching, and you haven't hit the middle rings yet.'

'You were watching me?' She tried for indignant and failed. She was a little bit thrilled that he cared enough to be there, focusing on her. 'Anyway, I'm only losing against myself.'

'Mmm. There's losing, and there's losing with humiliation,' Leo suggested lazily. He leaned against the wall casually, as if he hadn't a care in the world. Which was probably true, Amelia thought. He was the master of Grenville, a man at the top of his own world. But she didn't have to let him have it all his own way.

'Don't you have work to do?' she asked boldly.

He raised one eyebrow very slowly as if perfectly aware that she was provoking him. A shiver tickled her spine when the memory surfaced of his lips on hers; of how he could make her melt with a single touch. Okay, he had control of her in that way. But somehow that was all right — more than all right. If only . . . She stopped right there. If only he'd kiss her again. She shook her head, then realised he was looking at her with considerable amusement. She flushed. Was it obvious where her thoughts had taken her?

'Well?' she said with asperity, taking control herself. 'Work, Leo?'

'I'm having an enforced rest. The weather today hasn't permitted much estate work. So, I'm free to help you improve your darts skills.'

Before she could argue, he'd moved swiftly behind her and clasped her hand in his. He raised it with the dart in her fingers and moved her gently but firmly so that they faced the faraway board. She felt the warm caress of his breath on her hair; the heat of his body on hers; the strength of his broad shoulders as he stood so close to her. His fingers angled hers on the dart. The touch of them made her nerves vibrate like a wire strung too tightly.

'Ready?' he whispered.

She didn't trust her voice. She nodded. This wasn't helping her darts skills one little bit. She had no idea of the board or the trajectory of the dart as he sent it sailing across the room. She was only conscious of Leo — his strength and height; his scent and touch; the weird effect he had on the air around her, and on her body's responses.

Leo's clapping roused her from her daydreams. 'Well done, Amelia. You did it. You hit the bull's eye.'

'I did?' She saw her dart on the red

dot in the centre of the dartboard and grinned foolishly.

'You have a hidden talent after all,' he murmured in her ear. There was a wicked glint in his eyes.

'I was getting there by myself,' she said haughtily. 'With a bit more practice I'd have got it.'

He laughed. 'Come on now, be a good sport. Admit you need me.'

Amelia rolled her eyes. 'Okay, I need you.'

For a moment their gazes locked. Her chest tightened. *I need you.* Were need and want the same thing? Because she certainly *wanted* him. What was he thinking? His expression gave nothing away. She broke away from him with an effort.

'It's your turn,' she said sweetly, handing him the darts.

She watched Leo have a go. His aim was calm and true. There was confidence in how the dart sailed to the board and struck home — the confidence that Leo had in abundance. He was master of his own destiny.

And what of her destiny? It had been designed and moulded by William over so many years that it was hard to know how to deal with it all by herself. Yes, she was free now, or so it felt. But was she really? Her father cast a long shadow; she knew that from experience. Was he even now hunting her down? Did he know where she was, and who she was with? A cold shiver ran up her neck despite the heat. Was she never to be free of him; his power over her? What if . . . what if he found out she was at Grenville with Leo? Would he do it again? Her stomach creased with anxiety. She took the darts from Leo and threw them. One, two, three. They thudded to the floor aimlessly, far from the bull's eye. No matter.

'Excuse me,' she muttered.

'Amelia?'

She shook her head and brushed past him to leave.

Leo caught her arm. 'Tell me what it is. I can help you.'

'It's nothing. Really.' She managed a smile and left him there.

Inside her room, she pushed the door shut and leant against it. She didn't trust herself around Leo. Her want for him was so powerful. Could she really trust her heart? Did William's reach extend as far as Trinita? She'd had boyfriends like any normal girl. One or two had even touched her heart. One in particular she could have fallen in love with. But William had got rid of them all. They were unsuitable, he'd said, for a variety of reasons. So he bullied them out with his coldness and his lack of welcome, or he bought them off with bribes. She winced with embarrassment. She had had a price, as it turned out. A car for one would-be lover. A contribution towards university fees for another. And she had discovered that none of the men she chose wanted her enough to thwart her father.

What of Leo? He had no need of her father's wealth; he had his own. The master of Grenville was not a man to be bullied. So what would it take? A few choice words about Amelia's shortcomings? It had worked before.

She bit her lip and twisted her fingers until her knuckles hurt. She was being ridiculous. Leo didn't want her. Not truly. He was too caught up in his son and the hole in his life left by Grace. The pain shifted swiftly from her knuckles to the centre of her chest.

★ ★ ★

The heavy rain did not let up, and the air in the house became unbearably humid. Amelia's hair stuck to her forehead and her clothes felt clammy. She had a headache, which hadn't been helped by Lucio's roars and kicking feet as the baby woke up grumpy. Eventually he'd exhausted himself and had another nap.

Mora was the only member of the household seemingly unaffected by the weather. Efficiently she served up dinner to Amelia, Lucio having eaten earlier and been tucked up in bed. Amelia had been sure to put on the air conditioning in his room to combat the intense temperature, and now sat alone at the table while Mora bustled in and laid a plate of chicken salad in front of her.

'Is Leo coming for dinner?' Amelia asked. She hadn't seen him since Lucio's tantrum had driven him away.

'No, he asked to eat in his study.' Mora hesitated. 'Is there a problem between you two?'

'I don't think so,' Amelia said, not quite truthfully. 'Why do you ask?'

'It isn't like Leo to eat up there. He likes the ritual of a dinner, even on his own.' Mora sighed and shook her head. 'When Grace was here, in the early days, they always ate at six o'clock together with the full three courses, cutlery set out just right and so on.'

'Did you like Grace?' Amelia asked, curious.

Mora made a contemptuous noise in her throat. 'That woman deserves to be boiled in oil for what she did to this family. Look at us. We live inside these walls with alarm systems and monitoring, with Leo fretting all the while about the care of his son.' She smiled at Amelia. 'Though things have been changing since you got here, thank goodness. I never thought to see Leo let me take Lucio into town without him.'

'I'm glad I've been able to help,' Amelia said simply.

'You've helped, yes. Leo has become . . . very dependent on you, I'd say.'

'Leo, dependent on me? I don't think so. He's as stubborn as a rock. Nothing I say sways him at all. Sancia was right — he doesn't give way to others, as she put it.' The bread roll she'd taken broke into crumbs as she held it. She dropped it, then picked up her fork and put it back down.

'Sancia worries about him,' Mora said. 'It isn't good that he shuts himself away here. He works too hard and hardly socialises. It isn't healthy. So it's good you persuaded him to go to the barbecue last week.'

'Me? I didn't persuade him. He went because Joe and Neeva were back from America.'

Mora threw her a look. 'You think so? He didn't visit when Joe was over recently. No, he's changed. Whatever it is, it's a good change. We need you, Amelia. Grenville needs you.'

She bustled out, leaving Amelia with her mouth open. She knew why Leo was eating upstairs; he was unhappy with her for pushing him away. She picked up the fork, pushed her salad about and tried to eat some, without much success. She'd suddenly lost her appetite.

★   ★   ★

The screams jolted Amelia awake. She sat up in bed, disorientated, her heart thudding. The rain pelted against the window panes. It was pitch black, and her bed sheet was twisted around her. The screams came again. Lucio!

She stumbled from her bed, taking a moment to grab her thin silk dressing gown. If Leo was there, she did not want a repeat of the last time they'd met in the night. She ran along to the little boy's bedroom and pushed open the door. He was lying on his cot bed, squirming. She hugged him and soothed him. Behind her Leo arrived, his hair sticking up and his face creased with sleep.

'Is he all right?' he asked, joining her at the bed side.

'He needs his daddy,' Amelia said softly, moving aside so that Leo could cradle his son. She went downstairs to make warmed milk, tiptoeing carefully and hoping that Mora had slept through the noise. When she came back, Lucio was in Leo's arms. He was rocking his son, whose lids were heavy. With a shudder and a deep sigh, Lucio rolled over and fell asleep. Leo eased him back into his bed and drew up the cotton sheet to cover him lightly. The splatter of rain on glass grew louder.

'The rain must've woken him up,' Amelia whispered. She put the milk cup down on the bedside table.

'I feel completely helpless when he screams like that,' Leo said.

'But you did fine. You held him and soothed him.'

'I did fine because you were there. Since Grace left, I've been at a loss to know what to do with Lucio. I never felt this afraid before. To be single-handedly responsible for a tiny life . . . It's thrown me.'

'The master of Grenville, at a loss?' Amelia teased gently.

'Yes. Do you remember at the barbecue when I was perhaps a little harsh with you?'

'When I was talking to Wendy and Neeva? I was holding Lucio, and you practically snatched him from me to take him to his nana.'

'You noticed.'

'I wondered why you were unhappy with me.'

'It was unworthy of me, and I

apologise. It was . . . hard for me to see you with him. So natural and caring. You looked . . . *right* . . . together. And you were doing a better job than me at looking after my son.'

'You were *jealous* of me?' This was interesting. Suddenly his behaviour that day made sense: his annoyance with her; his withdrawal and sudden coldness. Amelia hid a smile. So the man who was so in control, who commanded this large house and estate, had been envious of her. She sort of liked it. Then she felt sorry for him. He was trying so hard to be a good father.

'Yes, I was jealous.' He sounded sheepish. 'You made caring for a baby seem easy.'

'Jealous.'

'Okay, don't go on about it. I admitted it. It wasn't right or good. It won't happen again.'

She moved a little closer. 'No, Leo, it won't happen again. Because you *are* good with him. You have no need to feel envious of me. You're wonderful with your son.'

She found it hard to make out his expression in the darkened room. The rain hit the windows with force.

'This sounds like a storm, but tomorrow will be a beautiful day,' Leo said, changing the subject abruptly.

'How do you know? I could believe it'll rain forever, hearing it now.'

'You forget, I've lived most of my life here. Trust me, tomorrow will be dry. The heavens will be emptied tonight and then there'll be a respite for a day or two.'

Amelia shivered despite the humid night. 'It's so different from the seasons in England.'

'Grace never got used to it. She never understood why I wanted to come back.'

'*Did* you want to come back? I got the impression from your mother that you came back out of duty to your father and the estate. That you were happy in London.'

He came round the side of the bed and stood by the window. The black night was illuminated only by the glazing sheets of water sliding down the glass. They glinted in the pale light from the room's nightlight.

'I was happy enough in London. I was in love with Grace, or thought I was. I imagined we'd live a life like Joe and Neeva — away most of the year but with an annual visit back to Grenville, to the family.'

'But Jose's illness changed all that,' Amelia prompted.

Leo shook his head. The nightlight caught the strong profile of his nose and chin. She waited for him to answer. Somehow it was easier to talk in the dark. There was no fear of waking the child. His soft snufflings were a comforting sound behind them.

'It changed even before my father's heart problems. Grace had no intention of travelling to Trinita every year. She didn't want to leave London at all. So we didn't come back, until my mother demanded it. Then we got married and came back here.'

'She must've loved you very much to agree to move here and leave London,' Amelia said hesitantly.

He made an impatient gesture. 'Grace loves only Grace. She was in love with the idea of marrying a rich estate owner. She didn't realise that it was forever; she thought she could persuade me to move back to London or New York. But when I came back, I knew this was where my life should be. Once Lucio arrived, that settled it. But when I saw how Grace neglected our baby in favour of her own selfish desires, I realised I had fallen out of love with her — or that I had been in love with an illusion, a version of Grace that she had projected for me to love.'

'I'm sorry,' Amelia said.

'You don't have to be sorry.' There was a touch of humour to his tone. 'You weren't there. It wasn't your fault.'

'That wasn't what I meant,' she said, turning towards him and seeing the shadows flicker and stretch on the walls. 'It's sad that it turned out that way, for you and Lucio — and Grace too.'

'You're too kind-hearted, Amelia Knight,' Leo said softly. 'You feel too much. You hear my depressing past and your heart aches for all of us despite our shortcomings. Grace did bad things, but I'm to blame too. I should never have brought her here. Perhaps somewhere there was a compromise I could've made for her if I'd loved her enough.' He shrugged.

The rain trickled blackly down the windows. It was easing off slightly. Amelia smiled; Leo's prediction was coming true. It might be dry the next day.

'What's making you smile?' Leo asked.

'Look, the rain's easing off. It must be your magic. Maybe I'll get a dry few hours for my day off.'

'I gave you a day off?' He pretended to be shocked.

'Actually, you didn't. Mora did.'

'And what are you going to do with your day off, Amelia?'

'I have no idea. If you can lend me a car, I might venture into town.' Although the thought of driving a vehicle along the track shot a bolt of panic through her stomach.

'I have a better idea,' Leo said. 'If you want, I'll take you to the most beautiful spot on our estate. We have a summerhouse with fabulous views, though it's a bit of a hike.'

She hesitated. She didn't want Leo to feel he had to spend the day with her — even if it gave her a ripple of excitement at the thought of spending time with him. Was he simply being polite?

'You don't have to,' he said quickly when she didn't speak. 'Forget it. I forgot you don't like the insects here, and it was crass of me to suggest that after your experience at the waterfall.'

'No, wait.' She caught his arm as he turned to leave. 'I'm not Grace,' she whispered. Meaning that she didn't hate Trinita; that actually the concept of living here was growing on her, although it was unspoken, and undecided in her mind.

'No, you're not Grace.' His voice thrummed with emotion, but she didn't dare to analyse it. 'Tomorrow then?' he said.

'Tomorrow,' Amelia whispered.

10

When Amelia woke up, it was as if her mind had crystallised all her worries during the night and come up with an answer. She was going to stay in Trinita. It was sharp and clear and felt oh so right. She hummed a melody under her breath as she showered. It was as if a weight had lifted from her chest. Thanks to the generous wage that Leo paid her, she had *options*.

Her contract as nanny here at Grenville would run out in a few short months. But that didn't mean she had to leave the island. If Leo wouldn't let her stay, she'd find other work nearby. There was no way she was going to abandon Lucio entirely. And his father . . . ? She rinsed off the citrus body wash and stepped out of the shower to dry off. She neatly evaded answering that question. The thought of Leo made her dress quickly. After breakfast they were going to the summer-house.

She looked up and almost screamed. A long black insect crawled towards her along the bathroom floor. She stared at it. It moved slowly and sinuously on hundreds of rippling legs. She took a deep breath. Willing her hand not to shake, she squeezed her eyes shut and lifted it. Its body was hard and scaly. She felt its legs whirring against her skin. She was nauseous. Opening her eyes, she walked firmly to the window, slid it up a fraction and let the creature out on the window ledge.

With a shudder she washed her hands. There. She had dealt with it. One goal to Amelia, nil to the wildlife! After that, she could deal with anything the jungle threw at her today. She hoped.

★ ★ ★

'Good morning, Amelia. Are you ready to hike?' Leo was dressed in casual work trousers and a khaki shirt. His jaw was freshly shaved and his hair slightly damp from his shower. Amelia had to swallow twice before she could answer. The urge to reach out and touch the slight curl of his hair, or to run her fingers along his jaw line and feel the roughness under her skin, was almost unbearable.

Instead, she spoke lightly as if unconcerned. 'Absolutely. Mora's lent me a pair of hiking boots, and I've got a sun hat and lotion. I'm looking forward to it.'

'Me too.' His smile set her senses wheeling. She focussed on eating the toast and jam that Mora put in front of her and drank two cups of tea to steady her jangling nerves. Spending a whole day with Leo was going to be exhilarating. She prayed she wouldn't disappoint him by tripping up or getting tired. Surely the summerhouse wouldn't be too far away?

'Okay, let's get our packs. We've a fair distance to cover before we can stop and eat our picnic.'

She groaned silently. So much for her hope. She pasted on a bright smile. 'Lovely. I'll be down in five.'

* * *

Mora and Lucio waved from the veranda. Amelia waved back enthusiastically. Beyond, Leo waited at the edge of the rainforest. He looked every inch the hunter, his khaki clothes blending in with the forest's green colours. His lithe, dark looks reminded her as ever of the panther waiting tense and ready. His golden eyes were lit with mischief as she turned from the house and took a deep and steadying breath.

'Are you prepared for an adventure?' he asked her playfully.

'Um, I think so . . . '

He laughed. 'You don't sound so sure. Come on, it's going to be fun, I promise you.'

'How long did you say the journey was?'

'I didn't. But we'll walk for a couple of hours only. It's not far.'

Not far — ? Amelia didn't think she'd ever walked solidly for two hours. Yet Leo said it casually as if it was nothing. Well, she wasn't going to let him see how daunted she felt. She slung her rucksack on and strode in front of him. 'Great, let's get going.'

It was easy at first, because all she had to do was follow the path. She heard Leo's measured footfalls behind her as he let her lead. She had nothing to fear while he was there. He was a solid and reassuring presence. Soon, however, they reached a fork in the path. She paused. The right fork went off towards the waterfall. She shuddered, remembering how that journey had ended. Her ribs were thankfully completely healed. She'd been lucky to escape with only bruises.

'I'm guessing we go left?' she said, wrinkling her nose with uncertainty.

He reached out and touched the tip of her nose briefly. 'No stressing,

Amelia. We're safe here. This is all my land. We can't go wrong. I know it all like the back of my hand.'

'But I don't. What if . . . what if you fell or hit your head or something, how would I get back to get help?'

He laughed a real Leo laugh, deep and throaty. *Sexy.* She shifted away. It was bad being too close to him — as if she'd reach out and pull him to her without being able to stop herself.

'You have a great imagination,' Leo said, his mouth quirking. 'Believe me, even if that happened, you'd be fine. I trust you to save me and get me home.'

'Now you're teasing me.'

'Maybe a little bit. But seriously, you worry too much.'

'Sorry.'

'And you say 'sorry' too much.'

Amelia grimaced. 'Yeah, sorry about that. See, there I go again. It's a bad habit from living with William. It was always easier to be the one to apologise and defuse the situation, even if I didn't feel I was in the wrong.'

Leo leaned in towards her. 'You don't live there anymore. You're here now, so you don't need to be sorry. About anything.'

Why was his gaze so mesmerising? She could lose herself in those golden pools like warm honey. And why not? Suddenly she couldn't think of a reason not to give in to her intense attraction to him. She'd held off because he was her employer. She'd been afraid to lose the security of this job. Let's face it, she'd needed the position desperately, with only a one-way plane ticket and no way home. But now . . . well, she had money put by, in the knowledge that this was a brief contract. Her fear of William influencing Leo now seemed foolish. She was thousands of miles from home. She was in Trinita, where, however much it hurt to leave Leo and Lucio, she wouldn't be far away. So why not give in to her desire for him?

She was leaning in to him without knowing it, until he drew back abruptly. It felt like a slap of icy water to her face.

Humiliated, she followed him along the left-hand path. Neither spoke. What had just happened back there? Had she totally embarrassed herself? Did he realise her intention?

He stooped down on the path so fast she almost stumbled over him. 'What . . . what is it?' She righted herself and looked about to see what had drawn his attention.

'These.' He held up three pieces of stone.

'What are they?'

'Put your hand out,' he commanded.

She could've taken issue with his tone; but now she knew him so well, it suddenly didn't feel like he was bossing her about. It was just Leo's way — to the point. It didn't mean he was trying to be in control of her. There was a freedom in realising that. She *liked* him. *Come on, Amelia, admit it. You like every little thing about him.*

She opened her palm and he laid the stones there. They felt heavy and cold. 'What are they?' she asked again. They were thin and heart-shaped, like tiny tokens of affection. For a wild second, she thought he'd given them to her for that reason. *Crazy, Amelia.*

He explained that they were stone-age arrowheads left behind by the first inhabitants of Trinita. She was intrigued.

'Wow, that's cool. How are they still here?'

Leo's face was intense and enthusiastic as he described the history of the island and the artefacts that had been found there. In turn, Amelia found she was genuinely interested. The stones were fascinating, but Leo was even more so. She'd no idea he was a history geek. He made the best-looking professor she'd ever listened to. If he'd presented on the History Channel she'd have been glued to it.

'Amelia?'

'What?'

'Did you hear a word of what I said?'

'Of course. The arrowheads are . . . Well anyway, when did you get into all this?' She had turned the question neatly back to him.

A corner of his mouth drew up. So he knew what she was doing. But she was more interested in what made him tick than in the old stones.

'They're part of the island.' He shrugged. 'A very ancient part. Think of it. We've been here for a mere blip of time, while these have lain undiscovered for thousands of years — until we walked here.'

'Wait a minute. You found them on the path, so they were hardly hidden.'

'So practical. You're right. Last night's heavy rain has washed them out of the soil. So you see, nothing stays the same. Even an arrowhead hidden for centuries must be exposed. Change, all things change.'

'Change isn't bad. You make it sound depressing.' She passed the tiny stones back to him. Their fingers met and retracted, like touching a burning candle. Too dangerous.

'In my experience, change is rarely

good,' Leo said quietly.

'You mean Grace leaving you?' Amelia asked bluntly.

'Possibly.'

Now she was exasperated. Was he never to move on? Had Grace blighted him forever, preventing him from loving any other woman? She froze. No, she hadn't meant that. She wasn't in love with Leo. But she did want a chance to explore what he could mean to her.

'What about Lucio?' she asked him. 'Wasn't that change when he was born? But that must've been one of the best events of your life.'

'Yes, that's true. I don't regret that. How could I?'

'So you have to agree with me then, change isn't always bad. How would we ever move on from bad experiences without change?' He grinned. 'What's so funny?' She shook her head. One minute they were having a deep heart-to-heart chat, and the next he was finding the whole thing wildly amusing.

'Sorry. It's just — if you could see

yourself . . . You've got your hands on your hips and your chin held high, as if you want to challenge me to a fight. I don't think you need to worry about being controlled. It's clear who's boss around here.' His tone was gently teasing.

Amelia relaxed her pose. It was unconscious. She smiled back at him. And in that moment she knew that William's influence over her was gone. She didn't care one whit what he thought; she wasn't going back. Even if she did, somehow his power to hurt her had vanished. Now she cared more what Leo's opinion of her was. Not whether he could take power over her life; that was never going to happen. No, she simply wanted him to admire her. Or more.

'I don't want to fight you,' Amelia murmured.

'That's good,' Leo said. 'I don't want to fight you either. You might win.'

'Would that bruise your male ego?' she mocked.

'Letting a mere slender stem of a girl beat me? I guess so.'

'What about equality of the sexes?' She was only half-joking now.

'Ahh, but Amelia, I'm an old-fashioned sort of guy,' Leo said. 'I like my women in the kitchen. I like to be the boss, you know.'

She couldn't help it. Raising up on tiptoe, she brushed a kiss on his jaw. *Let him see who's boss.* His reaction was swift. His eyes darkened and he caught her.

'Are you going to finish that?' he said in a low voice that made the tiny hairs on her neck rise. 'Never start something you're afraid to finish.'

'I'm not afraid.' Her heartbeat was racing. She wasn't afraid exactly, but it felt dangerous. Her mouth connected with his and his response was as fierce as her own.

Leo was the first to pull away. She felt the loss of his nearness. Her breath was coming fast. Did he regret it? The look on his face wasn't encouraging.

'Come on,' he said roughly. 'We should get going. Not far now.'

What was she doing? Leo wondered as he brushed past the glossy leaves that hung over the path. His body's physical response to Amelia still pulsed. Angrily, he slashed at the vines. She'd provoked him, but he'd done as much by telling her to finish what she'd started. Why the hell had she kissed him? What was she trying to prove? That she had the power to make his body react to her? Proven. That her kisses left him weak? Proven. But it was wrong. A big mistake. Giving in to their mutual attraction would only lead to sorrow for them both.

They had given in to it at the barbecue. But he knew there could be no happy ending. He'd sworn after Grace left never to leave his heart unguarded again. Any relationship now could be physical only.

He risked a glance at Amelia. Would she be content with that? Get it out of their systems. Let this madness go.

What did she want from him? What was he willing to give?

She was pointing with a delighted smile. 'Look, it's the summerhouse.'

He looked up and saw she was right; they had arrived. His own sense of pleasure in this place was expanded by hers. Amelia's grey eyes were bright as she brushed past him and ran to the wooden steps.

'This is beautiful!' she shouted back at him over her shoulder. 'Really gorgeous.'

And so are you. The words shot into his brain, unasked for. Her fair hair swung loose around her flushed face, and her slender waist was accentuated by the bush shirt tucked into her borrowed trousers. Her face showed all her emotions so clearly. How he had ever doubted her when she first arrived, he couldn't remember. She was so transparent. With Amelia Knight, what you saw was what you got.

The summerhouse was a construction of tropical hardwood with stairs leading up to a wide and open veranda. The view from there was spectacular: a panorama over the treetops and out to the wide estuary and the ocean beyond.

Amelia ran up the steps ahead of him, giving him a view of her rear. Womanly curves and then slim legs. 'Ohh, Leo, look at this!' she called down, her face alight.

He reached her in two loping strides, and grinned. There were birdfeeders strung from the summerhouse's roof. Near each of them, a hummingbird hovered like a shimmering jewel in turquoise and green, with a copper burnish.

'They are exquisite, aren't they?' he agreed.

She lifted her face, and her smile was so happy that something shifted inside him. Never mind what was right or wrong. He wanted her. And he knew she wanted him, too. Why not give in to it?

'Amelia,' he said, and his voice came out gritty as if his throat was sore.

She didn't speak; and as his hands reached for her, she came in to him and tilted her face so that he easily bent to find her lips.

He didn't ask her. He let his body do the asking, adjusting her body so that it fit to his. Her breath was sweet, and her light flowery scent enveloped him as his lips parted hers. His tongue sought and found hers. Her breathing was fast and shallow. Her breasts pushed against him with each inhalation. It struck a fire in his very centre.

He trailed hot kisses from the corner of her soft mouth and along the smoothness of her jaw, then down her neck. She made a moaning sound that pulsed his desire. He unbuttoned her shirt and slipped a hand inside. Then they were on the bed of leaves on the veranda floor, and neither cared about their surroundings.

The blood was rushing in Amelia's ears until she could only hear her breath. She didn't care anymore about whether they should or should not do this. She needed him. She desired him. She couldn't stop. Her body's responses were almost instinctive now, her mind no longer functioning. Through the mist of her pleasure, she heard his voice calling her name.

11

She was walking home surrounded by a warm glow. Her feet on the softness of the forest floor felt light like feathers. Like she was almost hovering above the surface of the ground, lifted by her exhilaration at their lovemaking. She felt again the touch of Leo's skin on hers. The memory was so real she could feel him. She glanced ahead to where he led the way, wondering what he was thinking. She might not be able to read his mind, but she knew now precisely how his body matched to hers; the special magnetism that clicked them together and couldn't be denied.

She tried not to over-guess what would happen next. Something magical had occurred, and she wanted to wallow in it; live it over; tease it out like wisps of cotton. There was a tiny stream not far from the path. The water channelled, rippling fast before splitting into two slim ribbons that bent in different directions. She imagined she was like the water — carried along, going where she would be taken this afternoon by their passion. Was it a casual affair, a brief meeting of bodies? She didn't believe that. It wasn't Leo's style, or her own. But what, then? What would they offer each other?

She followed one leg of the stream to where it ended, in a sinkhole in the forest floor. Great. If she took that analogy to the end, it didn't help. She screwed up her eyes against the sun to see where the other leg of the stream went. It fell off a scattering of rocks and vaporised in spray. *Well done, Amelia. Excellent choices.*

Forget the water. Forget comparing what they had done with anything. She was divided too. Did she want a serious love affair with Leo, a man who promised nothing? A man with serious ex-wife issues. Didn't she long for her independence, a chance to stand on her own at last — to prove to William that she had it in her to win, whatever he thought? *Note to self. I don't care what he thinks. Remember?*

But it was hard all the same to let it all go; to let the bad stuff vaporise like the stream water. The thoughts crowded her head. Then she saw them: two gleaming jewels in the leaf litter. Bright red and green, like rubies and emeralds. Curious, she stretched out a hand to pick them up. Leo grabbed her and pulled her back. Amelia's heart ran double-time with shock.

'No, don't touch those! For God's sake, don't you know anything?'

'Stop grabbing me like that. What on earth are you doing?'

'You really don't know?'

'Know what? Quit speaking in riddles. What's the matter? What are those things?'

'Dart frogs. They're so steeped in venom that one touch can be fatal.'

She drew in a quivery breath, hardly believing him. The pulse in her neck fluttered. 'Really? They look like cute little frogs with happy colours.' She saw them better now: not jewels but miniature creatures, sort of rubbery like a couple of bath toys.

'I showed you the arrowheads on the way in. The natives have been using these creatures for years to tip their weapons. Once the arrow hits an animal, it dies instantly from the venom.'

'Okay, now you're scaring me.'

'You should be scared. Trinita is a dangerous place.'

Her pulse went haywire. It was dangerous all right, but not just in the way he meant. He was standing so close to her — protectively close. She inhaled his scent. All man. All Leo. She had an urge to reach up and touch the rugged line of his jaw, which was darkly bristling already as afternoon drew towards early evening.

'I survived the caiman and the ugly beetle. I've even held a . . . well I don't know what it was, but it had an awful lot of legs. So I'm sure I'd have survived the frogs.' *Keep it light. Don't let him see I'm shaken. No comparisons with Grace, please. Please.*

He shook his head, looking so exasperated that she wanted to kiss his displeasure away.

'One touch. That's all. Grace never understood the power of this place either. Maybe you English can't. There's no wildlife that can harm you there.'

Grace. Was it really possible to dislike someone so much whom she'd never met? She was suddenly angry at the comparison. 'I do get it. I get the fact that Trinita is tropical; that it's full of . . . weird stuff that I don't know about. Yet. But I'll figure it out. I will. Just because I'm English and blonde like your ex-wife does not mean I'm like her in other ways. Give me a chance. Leo?'

He was like stone; not swayed by her argument at all, it appeared. And he'd ruined the mood. The last person she wanted mentioned right now was

Grace; not after the wonder of the afternoon in the summerhouse. Just her and Leo. Not Grace. Not William. No one else to shred at their doubts, their emotions. She had enough doubts now all by herself. Perhaps Leo was incapable of moving on. Perhaps she was, too? All her bold statements that she was done with her father, that she didn't care what he thought — were they true?

She stared at the glowing jewels that were so deadly. She would have touched them. She might have died, if not for Leo. What else was out here in this alien place? And was she really up to living here? Her skin felt thin; vulnerable. Her certainty fell away, and her joy in the day, to be replaced by all the old fears and anxieties.

'Come on,' Leo said. 'We should get going. Night falls fast out here. If it's not the dart frogs, it'll be the leopards that get you.'

'That's a joke, isn't it?'

'Sort of. There are leopards. But they

have yet to eat anyone. Get your rucksack. And please, Amelia, avoid touching any of the wildlife. Promise me?'

'I'm only too glad to agree. Will we make it back before it's dark?'

'We will if we walk now. You don't need to worry; I'm not going to leave you.'

Their eyes met. Leo was the first to look away. He shouldered his pack and led them back to the path.

They didn't talk much after that, and Amelia simply followed Leo's tall figure through the trees until they reached Grenville. It didn't strike her that he was quiet. In fact, she didn't get a chance to think about it at all, because waiting on the step when they returned was William Knight.

She was strangely unsurprised to find him there. Of course he had hunted her down. The only surprise was that it had taken so long. Her first impression was that he was grown smaller, somehow. He was a good inch shorter than Leo.

Her father had always loomed large in her mind, but now he didn't have the same impact. Amelia forced a smile. 'This is unexpected. Why are you here?'

'You rather pushed my hand when it came to my travels this summer.' His cold blue eyes assessed her. 'I'm here to see whether you've come to your senses yet and to bring you home.'

Amelia sensed rather than saw Leo step to her side. Before she could speak, he had cut in politely but firmly.

'Why don't you show your father inside, Amelia. We can continue this conversation in comfort. I'll ask Mora to bring some refreshments.'

William inclined his head. 'That's very kind of you. I should've phoned ahead to say I was intending to drop in, but mobile reception is poor.' His tone implied criticism of Grenville as if Leo were solely responsible for the problem.

'No worries. If you'd like to stay for a few days that can be easily arranged.' Leo guided them both into the house. The perfect host.

'There's no need for that,' William told him. 'I won't be staying and neither will my daughter.'

Amelia was stunned. Only the presence of Leo and Mora kept her from arguing with him right there and then. If he thought she was meekly going to follow him back to England, he could think again!

Leo caught her on her own in the kitchen, where she'd gone to fetch in cutlery. Mora hadn't stopped her. The older woman knew she needed a moment to compose herself.

'Do you want me to stay here with you?' Leo asked. 'I was intending to go over to see my parents, but I don't have to go today.'

She hesitated. It was tempting. With Leo beside her, she'd have back-up and the comfort of his solid strength. But she had to face William at some point. Better now, when she was in a position of strength. She had a job and a place to live. She had people she cared about. She had Leo.

'No,' she said, shaking her head. 'You should go see your parents. I need to speak to William alone.'

'Are you sure?'

She looked at him and saw the concern written on his face. Her heart did a little flip. She had come to rely on Leo, even if they'd messed up by making love. It hadn't changed the fact that they were . . . friends. If she asked him to stay, he would. She sighed.

'No, I'm not sure. I'm not sure of anything right now. But it's better if you go. William and I have to sort things out. It's been a long time coming.'

He nodded. 'If you need me, I'll come back. Okay?' He lifted her chin with one finger and looked straight at her.

She fought an impulse to cry. *Pathetic, Amelia. The man is tender with you and you want to wail like a baby. Not only wail, but press against his broad chest and let him protect you from the world. Get some backbone,* she chided. So she took a deep breath and turned partly away from him. 'Go, Leo,' she said softly. 'I'll be fine, really.'

She listened to his footfalls as he moved across the hall, and then heard the sound of the car engine as he drove out of the yard. Only then did she make her way back to the living room to find her father.

He was standing there looking out of the wide veranda window, his back to her. Mora had discreetly vanished. There was a plate of small cakes, a pot of coffee and two cups waiting on the low table. A couple of scattered toys lay under it. Amelia wished it was an ordinary day and that she were playing with Lucio. How simple life was when there were daily tasks. Instead, she had to confront William.

'So this is where you ran to.' He didn't bother to turn to her as he spoke.

'How did you find me?' she asked.

He turned now, unsmiling. 'I found the job advertisement in your room. I must admit I was surprised, on enquiring, to find that you'd been successful in gaining the work.'

So he'd had his man investigate her. William kept a private investigator on retainer as part of his business dealings. She'd never asked why.

'You were surprised because you thought you'd made it impossible for me to get a nanny position.'

He calmly took a seat at the table and indicated that she should join him. Biting the inside of her lip, she sat. She would not give him the satisfaction of losing her temper.

'You know that I only have your best interests at heart,' he said. 'Why don't you pour the coffee?'

Amelia was pleased that her hand did not shake as she lifted the ceramic pot. Mora had made the coffee hot and strong. She filled the two cups and passed him one politely. She'd play the game; be civilised. If she felt like screaming, she would think of Leo, and it would calm her.

'My best interests?' Her voice rose a little and she tamped it down. 'My best interests,' she repeated quietly. 'I'm old enough to know what I want.'

'You've always known what you want,' William agreed, 'but that's not to say it's what is right for you.'

His sheer arrogance made her gasp. Yet, why was she surprised? He hadn't changed, and was never going to. But she had. Travelling to Trinita and finding Leo and Lucio had made her more confident and sure of herself. And there was no way she was letting William take that away from her.

'What gives you the right to meddle constantly in my life?' she said angrily.

'I'm your father.'

'But I'm not ten years old anymore. I'm not a little girl who can be sent away from home at the snap of your fingers.' She put down her cup. Her hand was now shaking too much to hold it. So much for not losing it with him!

'I sent you to boarding school for your own good. I gave you the best education money can buy, and look at

215

how you've wasted it — on jobs that are going nowhere.'

'What about my happiness? Isn't that more important?'

He made a noise in his throat, then lifted his coffee cup deliberately and drained it. It landed back in the saucer with a loud, distinct clink. 'You'd be happier working for me in the bank. That's a secure job with good prospects. What you fail to realise, Amelia, is that you have to plan for the future. Where do you want to be in five years' time? Surely not working as a childminder in someone else's house, at their beck and call like a maidservant?' His voice dripped with derision.

'Leo treats me well. I'm not at his beck and call, as you put it. I enjoy looking after his son and am helping him grow up into a happy and contented little boy. Whatever you say, it's worthwhile. And . . . ' She paused, then added simply, 'It's who I am.'

'You think you know these people?' William said. 'I know Leo Grenville.

I've had business dealings with him. Don't get yourself in too deep, Amelia.'

'What do you mean?'

'His reputation precedes him, that's what.' William sneered. 'He styles himself the master of Grenville and he dominates it like an old-fashioned tyrant. He won't brook any dissent from his family or workers, and he's a bully.'

'And you got all this from meeting him in London?' Amelia enquired sarcastically.

William's cold blue eyes widened at her tone. He wasn't used to her talking back. It gave her some brief satisfaction before his next words.

'No, I got it from his wife, Grace Grenville.'

For a moment she was speechless. 'You've met Grace?'

'Grace lives in London and moves in the same circles as I do, shall we say.'

'They aren't married anymore,' Amelia said. 'And there are reasons why Grace Grenville would want to blacken Leo's name. He's certainly not a bully. He's kind and considerate to everyone and extremely loyal to his family. You've been misinformed.'

William raised an eyebrow. 'Indeed. You seem very passionate in his defence. I'm curious. How long have you known him?'

'Long enough to know that Grace is lying about him.' It made her sick to think of Leo's ex-wife spreading malicious stories about him. Presumably she wasn't sharing the fact that she'd neglected her own child, or that she had abandoned him finally for her own selfish pleasures.

'Be that as it may,' William said, 'I've booked your ticket back to London. You must know that this can't last. Let's look at it as a summer job. You can fly back in a couple of months' time, when you've got it out of your system, and there'll be a place waiting for you in my office.'

It was almost funny, how conceited and self-centred he was. He hadn't listened to her at all. He never had. Hot tears welled up under Amelia's eyelids and she had to squeeze them away. 'When I saw you standing on the porch,' she said quietly, 'for a moment . . . I really thought you'd come to see me. That you'd missed me. Maybe even that you were proud of me for travelling here to the tropics and finding a place to live.' She shook her head. 'But I was wrong. Like I've been wrong about you my whole life. It's never about me; it's all about you. You want me back in the bank in London because that'll reflect well on you to your business associates. Family is so important in your circles, isn't it? Or at least, how it looks on the surface. But the truth is, William, I'm not coming back. Not now. Not ever.' She stood up, hiding her fists in the pockets of her bush trousers. Her nails bit into her palms. It helped.

'Amelia . . . ' he began in the same weary tone he used when she was being particularly obstinate in his opinion.

She pulled her hand from her pocket

and held it palm-up in front of him. He stopped, surprised. 'Not this time,' she said bleakly. 'I'm sorry, but you've had a wasted journey.' She showed him to the door. He took a step outside and then looked at her.

'You'll regret this.'

She shook her head. 'I don't think so. In fact, I've never felt so certain about anything in my life before.'

He smiled, but there was no humour or love in it. 'I wish you well of him.'

'Leo?' She wasn't sure what he meant.

'You're in deeper than I imagined. You fancy yourself to be in love with him. Take care, Amelia. As the saying goes, be careful what you wish for.'

Before she could protest that he was wrong, William Knight stepped out into the yard. His mobile was already pressed to his head and she heard him call a town taxi. The mobile reception was working for once and she was relieved he didn't have to linger.

His final words echoed in her head.

He was wrong. She wasn't in love with Leo. Of course she wasn't. How could she love a man who was still hurting from his ex-wife's betrayal? They might be able to be friends, or even casual lovers, but there was no future in loving Leo.

The events of the day crashed in on her abruptly. She ran inside and upstairs, then fell onto her bed and allowed the hot tears to fall.

★ ★ ★

Sancia opened her arms to her eldest son with a welcoming smile. 'Leo, how lovely to see you. Come and speak to your papi. He's got a plan to renovate the walled garden, silly man. It's too much for him. Too much.' She looked behind him as she spoke. 'Where's Amelia? Didn't I tell you to bring her with you next time you visited?'

'She's busy, Mama,' Leo said. 'So, what can I do to help?'

But Sancia wasn't letting him off that

easily. Her dark eyes narrowed. 'What's going on? Something's happened between the two of you. I know it.'

'No, nothing's happened.'

'So she's working today? Looking after my *bebe*?'

'Not exactly.'

'Aha.' Sancia's voice was triumphant. 'She's not working, so she can be here, yes?'

'Mama, please can you let it go, just this once?'

Her voice softened in concern. 'What is it? Are there problems? She's such a nice girl.'

Leo sighed. He hugged his tiny mother with a wry grin. 'The only problem is your tenacious matchmaking. Believe me, it's all in your imagination.'

She threw him a knowing glance. 'We'll see.'

'Where's Papi?' Leo asked. 'I'll give him a hand in the garden. Do the heavy lifting.'

'You know, Leo, it's time you moved

on. Let the past go.'

His mouth tightened. His mother was echoing Mora's advice, but he didn't want to hear it. The trouble was, she was still speaking. When Sancia Grenville bit into a subject, she was terrier-like.

'Don't you want a brother or sister for Lucio? Do you want him to be a lonely only child?'

'He isn't lonely. He has me and Mora . . . and his nanny.'

'You won't even name her? Don't think I don't know why. You get rid of them so easily. You think it's better for Lucio that way. But I'm not so sure. You can't protect him from everything life will throw at him.'

'I can try.'

'If he had brothers, they'd look after each other through life. Look at you and Daniel and Joe. Three strong men who are there for each other. Am I right?' Her voice lifted at the end in emotion.

She was right. Leo and his brothers

were close. Growing up, they had each other's backs. With a pang, he thought of Lucio. There was no large family to buffer him from all the heartache and trials as he grew. Leo had sworn to do that all by himself. Now he began to wonder if it were possible.

'Look at Kenny and Lara.' Sancia wasn't giving up. 'How good they are together.'

'They fight like cat and dog,' Leo said drily.

'Yes, yes.' She shrugged her shoulders. 'Of course they do. Brother and sister, it's natural. But if anyone else tries to bully one of them, the other fights for them. You see? It's about family. And what about you? It's not just Lucio I worry about. Do you want to spend the rest of your life alone?'

Did he? It was what he deserved. It was punishment for failing Lucio, and Grace too. The blame did not lie entirely with her. He was at fault for marrying her and bringing her to Trinita, where she didn't belong.

Then Amelia sprang into his mind. She was never far from it. She had settled on the island as if she'd lived here for years. Yes, she had battled with the insects and climate, but she'd come through. He was proud of her. Ridiculously so, given he had no claim to her. Their lovemaking in the summerhouse had been an error of huge proportions. He blamed himself. It had not been an honourable action. He wondered how, or if, he could ever make it up to her. How he could let her down gently.

'Do you?' Sancia prompted.

'That's how it is,' he said simply.

She made an impatient movement with her hands. 'Take control of it. Make it happen.'

Take control. Something Amelia couldn't abide, he thought with a smile. He wondered how her conversation with William was going. What if she'd left with him? There was a hollowness in the pit of his stomach at the thought. She couldn't go. Not yet. Not while he had things to discuss with her. He had to have time to make it right, although he had no idea how.

He was belatedly aware that Sancia had an air of repressed excitement. Surely not because of his visit? 'What is it, Mama? You're hiding something.'

'I wasn't supposed to tell you. But Joe knows I can't keep a secret.'

'Don't tell me, then.'

'I have to, or I'll burst. Only, don't tell Joe and Neeva that I told you.'

'Seriously, don't tell me. Let Joe if he wants to.'

'Neeva's pregnant!' The words burst out of her with pride and joy.

For an instant it was as if someone had pierced his chest with a knife, such was the searing and unpleasant sensation of jealousy he experienced. But it was unworthy of him. He had *never* been jealous of his little brother.

'That's wonderful news,' he managed.

'Isn't it? Neeva tells me they want a big family, at least four kids. In America there's space for them to grow. It's a big land and Joe has a sprawling house. They want to fill it with children.'

He was glad for them. He tried for humour. 'You see, Mama — Lucio will have thousands of cousins, which will make up for no brothers or sisters.'

'Don't think our conversation is over,' she warned. 'But for now, I'll take you to Papi and the pile of bricks that needs to be moved.'

As he lifted wheelbarrow-loads of dusty bricks, Leo's mind turned to Amelia. He had to make it right with her. His thoughts strayed. Was there any chance she was pregnant from their lovemaking? A baby with golden curls and big grey eyes was conjured by his mind. A little girl in the image of Amelia.

He threw down the heavy shovel and wiped his damp brow with his arm. Damn it, what was going on with him? It would be an utter disaster if there was a baby. She'd told him it was safe. It had to be.

12

After a restless night of wrestling with his conscience, Leo knew what he had to do. He had to tell Amelia why their passion at the summerhouse could not be repeated; why it had been a mistake. He dreaded it. But it was unfair to her — to both of them — to let her think anything could come of it.

There was something else. He picked up the short letter lying on the bedside table and frowned as he scanned the words once more. He was tempted to crumple the bitter text and throw it in the rubbish, but first he wanted to know more.

Which was why he couldn't put it off any longer. He went to find Amelia.

★ ★ ★

'I don't understand,' she said, bewildered. 'Forgive you for what?'

He shook his head. 'It was my fault. I gave in to my desire for you. But I can't . . . I can't offer you a commitment.'

'It takes two, Leo.' Amelia spoke calmly and slowly while her heart pounded fast with anger at his . . . his bull-headedness! 'I wanted this as much as you did. I'm not going to say sorry for . . . ' *Making love with you.* ' . . . for being together, which we both wanted.'

They were standing in the living room just beyond the exit to the veranda, alone. Mora had taken Lucio out. Outside, at the honey feeders, the hummingbirds fluttered like emerald jewels. They reminded Amelia of her fleeting happiness in the summerhouse. It had now been replaced by an anger that made her almost shake. 'I'm not ashamed of what we've done. Don't spoil it by apologising to me, for goodness sake!'

'But you do see that it can't happen again?'

'Not really, no.' She wasn't going to make this easy for him.

'Amelia . . . ' He looked at her.

She looked away. She couldn't bear the anguish that she saw there, and preferred to stoke the anger that kept her standing, ramrod-stiff. 'Look, Leo. If it was a mistake, then that's fine. We'll let it go and pretend it never happened,' she said, proud that her voice didn't shake. Her pride was the only thing she had left now; otherwise, humiliation would flood in. He couldn't be any clearer in what he was saying: making love with her had been a huge mistake. He didn't want her.

'Pretend it never happened?' he said softly. 'That's impossible. For both of us, I think.' He lifted her chin gently and looked deep into her eyes. There was pain in his. Her heart clenched. It took all her willpower not to touch him, to wipe away the emotion, to attempt to heal whatever ailed him. Instead she stared back and willed her anger to remain with her.

'That's what you want, isn't it? For this . . . episode . . . whatever you want to call it, to disappear.'

He gave a sigh that hollowed her out. 'It was a mistake.'

She winced. She deserved it. Hadn't she wanted plain speaking between them? But it still hurt. 'We'll put it behind us, then. Go on like it never occurred. If that's what you want.'

'What I want . . . ' He sounded angry and exasperated. 'What I want . . . It doesn't matter what I want. What matters is that you aren't hurt by this. By my . . . actions.'

Actions. He wasn't going to call it making love. That hurt more than anything. But Amelia was used to disappointment; to being pushed away to arm's length. She had coped with it most of her life. She could handle this. So what if her chest hurt with pent-up tears. So what if her jaw ached with keeping a lid on her emotions. She'd toughened up recently. She was strong. Hadn't Leo told her that?

'I'm not trying to hook you into a relationship,' she said bluntly. 'It was a bit of fun, that's all.'

'I don't believe you're like that,' Leo replied. 'And that's why it mustn't happen again. I don't want to be the cause of upsetting you. But I'm not ready, will never be ready to love again. I gave myself entirely to my ex-wife, and my trust and love were betrayed. I never want to feel that way again. And it wouldn't be fair to you if we began an affair, because there's a level of emotion, an intensity of it, that I cannot ever feel. For anyone.'

Grace. She was always there, even though absent physically. She was like a barrier between them, Amelia thought savagely. She had poisoned Leo's life; made it impossible for him to move on.

A sour thought hit her: William. Was it possible . . . ? Her throat was dry as she forced herself to form the words. 'Did he get to you?'

'Who?'

'My father. Did he talk to you before he left?'

She saw from Leo's face that he

understood. He pulled a sheet of crumpled paper from his pocket and gave it to her. She scanned it quickly, tainting her mind with the short text — that was what it felt like. Numbly, she returned it.

'It means nothing,' Leo said. 'It has no bearing on my decision.'

'Are you sure about that?'

He sighed heavily and moved instinctively towards her, but then froze and shook his head. When he spoke, his voice was gentle. 'Tell me about it.'

Amelia shrugged carelessly. The hurt burned her shoulder blades and prickled her eyes. But she would *not* give way to it. Not now. She was a different person from the frightened girl who had run from London. Right?

'My father . . . ' Her voice broke so she began again. 'My father has always vetted any man who has been interested in me. Are they good enough for his daughter? I don't mean are they kind, considerate, good people. I mean are they wealthy enough, socially connected enough to be the son-in-law of William Knight, CEO?' The paper in her hand felt damp. She smoothed out its wrinkles and folded it once, precisely. 'And what a surprise, none of them ever measured up.' A second fold, equally sharp. 'If a verbal warning didn't work, then an envelope of cash usually had the magic touch.' Fold, fold. Sharp crease. Razor edge. 'But a letter? He's reached new heights, sullying my name in his writing. Telling you clearly what a loser I am.' The letter was a tiny, hard square.

'Amelia,' Leo said softly, 'I'm sorry about your father. I am. But none of it matters. Okay? Let it go. Let him go. He's not worthy of you. Do you think I truly believe what he's written about you? Do you know me so little? I know you, Amelia Knight. I know what a wonderful, brave, independent woman you are. I'd never let this acid drip in my ear. Give it to me.'

She passed the paper to him. Their fingertips touched. All her yearning for him welled up. She stepped back and felt a strength coming from someplace deep within her. She was going to get through this: her father's rejection and now Leo's. Because that was what was going on. She was losing him, before she got a chance to try and see if they could make it work.

He dropped the paper into the small bin at the door and shut the lid. Gone — but not forgotten.

'I should go,' she said.

'What?' He sounded startled. 'Go where?'

'Don't you see, Leo?' she cried. 'I can hardly stay at Grenville. Seeing you every day, working beside you, after this. It's beyond awkward.'

The hummingbirds flew up, scared away by the noise. The feeders swung empty, as if the soul of the place had gone.

'Don't be silly. You mustn't go.' He paced the wooden floor. 'Lucio is making such good progress. You can't go.'

'Isn't it for the best?' she asked quietly. 'You said yourself, you don't want him getting attached to me. And what about us? Even if you won't find it awkward, I will.' *Because I still want to make love with you. Now even more than before.*

'It doesn't have to be.' He stopped in front of her. 'We'll make it work. Please don't leave, Amelia. I'll never forgive myself if I've driven you away. You must stay and work at Grenville. Please?'

How could she say no to such dark passion? 'Okay, I'll stay. Until my contract finishes. Happy?'

He didn't look it. But he nodded. 'Yes.'

The sun had strengthened and poured down on them, burning where it touched. Amelia knew already that this was going to test her, being there every day with Leo just out of reach. Her body was aching for him now. Was it possible that as the days went by, her desire would flicker and fade away if it wasn't fed by his touch? She could only hope so.

She looked up. He was still standing there, a dark and shadowed expression on his features. The tension between them was almost unbearable, and she had no idea how to ease it.

'Amelia, I have to ask you . . . '

'Ask me what?'

'You said it was safe,' Leo said slowly. 'I want to be sure . . . '

Did he think she'd lied? She turned to him. 'I told you the truth. It was safe.'

'I should've been prepared, had some protection with me.' His mouth twisted. 'But it was spontaneous. I hadn't planned on doing what we did.'

'No, it kind of engulfed us,' she agreed with a tentative smile. 'Besides, it's my responsibility too.'

He looked relieved. 'I don't wish to bring a child into this world that isn't wanted by both parents.'

'No.' But unbidden came the thought of a baby — Leo's baby. She wanted babies at some point. They'd always been part of her plan for the future. But here and now? He was probably right.

'Lucio was unplanned, as I told you,' Leo was saying. 'When I found out that Grace was pregnant, I was overjoyed. In my excitement I missed the fact that my wife wasn't happy. When she told me she didn't want the baby, I ignored what she was telling me. I thought, mistakenly, that she'd come round to the idea. I was happy enough for both of us. I believed I could carry all three of us forward into a rosy future.' He gave a bitter laugh.

Amelia wasn't sure she wanted to hear this. The pain in his voice was raw. It was as if a gate had opened. But he was speaking once more; there was no stopping him.

'Can you imagine how I felt the day I found her at the abortion clinic? She was booked in and sitting in the waiting room, calm and peaceful as if waiting for a routine check-up. No guilt or remorse. No tears. She was going to kill our child without a care. She hadn't considered my feelings or wishes.' His hands balled.

Amelia fought an urge to comfort him. 'That's so awful,' she said, feeling it an inadequate response to what he was describing.

'I talked her out of it and took her home. I thought . . . I thought if we spoke to each other, if we laid out what we felt, that we could work it through.'

'But she had the baby. She had Lucio,' Amelia said, 'so you got through to her.'

'At some level, I got through. She agreed to have him because I told her it was the only way we'd stay married. Grace liked her lifestyle. She wasn't ready to give up the master of Grenville and all it implied. So yes, she had Lucio. And you know the rest of the story — the neglect; her lack of interest in him. She refused to risk having any more babies. It was separate bedrooms from then on, and finally separate lives. No marriage can survive that kind of distance.'

Amelia's heart went out to him. Poor Leo. What a hell he'd lived in. 'You've done everything you can for Lucio. He's a healthy, happy little baby and he doesn't want for love,' she said.

'But when one day he asks about his mother, it'll be difficult. So you can understand why I won't bring another child into the world that doesn't have both parents there to love it. You of all people must see that, having lived with your father.'

There was a knot in her throat. She had experienced the unconditional love of her mother and then been left with a cold and distant father; a man who kept her at arm's length and finally pushed her right out of his life into boarding school. But she didn't care about that right now. All she cared about was Leo and his pain. The hollow feeling in her ribcage intensified, because she understood why he, too, was pushing her away.

Their lovemaking had not brought them closer; it had had the opposite effect. He had been through so much with Grace that Amelia saw he was incapable of letting himself try again with somebody new. He wouldn't risk it. And he wouldn't risk Lucio being unhappy in the future either. Amelia understood it, though she didn't have to like it. There was an insurmountable wall right there in the space between them, invisible and impossible to scale. So why did she feel like she wanted to keep on trying?

She didn't want a relationship either, Amelia reminded herself. She had only just won her freedom from William. She owed it to herself to be independent; to stand firmly on her own two feet, not to be in a twosome where she'd have to bow to another's wishes. So it shouldn't matter that Leo didn't want that either. She ought to be relieved. He'd called her strong. She wanted time to sample that strength; to be an individual, free from someone else's control.

Having thought it through, it ought to feel good. So why did she feel . . . let down, somehow? Lonely, rather than proudly alone. *Get a grip*. She inhaled sharply and tasted the sweet tropical air; let it jazz with her head. There, that was better. She thrust her shoulders back and lifted her head.

'I completely understand what you mean,' she told Leo. 'But you don't have to worry. I'm on the pill, so there won't be any problems.'

She said it almost casually. Did it mean she had a recent boyfriend back in England? Or that she was used to casual flings? Leo studied her as they cleared up the remains of their picnic. Her blonde curls were springy with the heat. They encircled her face like a golden halo. Her grey eyes were guarded. He felt a strange surge of protectiveness. He liked her better when her expression was open and relaxed. He hated that she was trying to hide what she was feeling, and all because of him.

He cursed inwardly. Making love with her at the summerhouse had been wonderful. He didn't want her to suffer because of it. Damn it. They had both lost their heads. The only regret he had was that he had hurt her by telling her he couldn't commit. It was the truth, and he wanted her to be under no illusions. But he'd hurt her, it was obvious. And now he didn't know how to put it right.

Telling her about Lucio's birth hadn't helped. What the hell was he doing? Digging a hole deeper and deeper. Not only had he told her he didn't want an affair, but that if she were pregnant it would be a disaster! Hardly the master of tact.

Leo rubbed his face. The thing was, he knew he was saying what had to be said. *But.* He liked Amelia Knight. The more he got to know her, the more he liked her. William Knight had missed out on someone special when he rejected his daughter's love.

She'd offered to leave. So why had he said no? Wasn't it the perfect answer? Especially when she was on a short contract anyway, at his own insistence. Mora had wanted to make it an open-ended contract, but he'd refused to do so despite her arguments. Now, ironically, he was the one telling her to stay. At least until the end of her few months' work.

'We . . . I have to make the daily checks on the estate.'

'Yes, of course. I'm sure you've got lots of work to do,' Amelia said with a brief smile that didn't brighten her eyes.

'Not so much today,' he replied. He had to keep her talking. Anything to get her animated again, so that he could get rid of the guilt that washed over him.

'Really? Can't you come up with some? I thought you were a workaholic.'

That was better. There was an edge to her voice that pleased him. A sharpness, like she might just want to lash out.

'I have been called that, and I do work hard on the estate. This last year,

244

work has been my medicine.' That was too honest. He didn't deserve the sympathy he saw now in her face. 'But as master of Grenville, I'm entitled to time off when I want,' he ended in a deliberately pompous manner.

As he hoped, the sympathy faded. Did she even know how open her expressions were? She'd be a disaster at poker!

'How lovely for you, to be able to work if and when you fancy it. Most of us have to grind away whether we feel like it or not.' Her voice was sharp and had an edge of criticism.

'But you love nannying, don't you?' he prompted her.

It had the desired effect. Her smile was genuine. 'Yes, I do. Cross out what I just said. I never feel it's a grind when I'm with kids. I love helping them and seeing them develop. If I ever feel tired, I only have to remember the holiday temping I did at William's bank.'

'So you did work for him, then?' Leo was surprised. 'I thought he tried to persuade you but failed?'

'He wanted me to work full-time at the bank, which I was never going to do. But yes, in the college holidays I did temp for him. I suppose I hoped that would be sufficient, and he'd be able to stop nagging me to go into banking. But it was so boring; I absolutely hated it.'

'It's good luck for Lucio and me that that was the case.' He injected a humorous tone into his words; a light touch. He wasn't sure of what she was thinking, or of how fragile she was after the events of this morning.

'And for me. This job has been a lifeline.' Her reply was heartfelt.

'And when it ends?' He braced himself.

'I don't know. Something will turn up.' She went out onto the veranda and paused to look back at him. 'Don't worry about it. I'm not your responsibility. It's up to me to sort out my life.' She softened it with a smile that didn't quite lighten up her eyes. The sun fell upon her browned skin and warmed it to the colour of honey.

A strange sensation shot through Leo. He couldn't name it. It was a mixture of dark thrill, sweetness and tender caress, all focused on the slender woman in front of him. Confused, he backed away with a swift turn to the main door and the wild jungle waiting for him.

13

She couldn't be. Amelia stared at herself in the bathroom mirror. Wide grey eyes stared back in a pale face. She dampened a face cloth and washed her mouth. Her hand shook. The nausea subsided as she counted days frantically in her mind. Her periods were as regular as clockwork. But she'd definitely missed one. It had been due a week after the summerhouse afternoon. She hadn't noticed it missing because she was busy with Lucio.

Mora had been ill, so Amelia had taken over the housekeeping duties too. Leo had been absent. He was working, it seemed, every hour of the day. When their paths did cross, he was polite and courteous, nothing more. Amelia cringed to think of how intimate they'd been. And now, it was like it had never happened.

Well, two could play at that. She was polite back to him, and their conversation over dinner was of weather and work and how Lucio was progressing. Inside, she stung badly, but pride would not let her ask Leo if he'd forgotten that day.

She groaned and cradled her stomach. She didn't need a test kit to know she was pregnant. She hadn't forgotten to take her pill, but she'd got confused with when to take them due to the time difference. Now she cursed. She should've been more careful. She and Leo . . . But she didn't, couldn't, regret that afternoon. Even with its devastating consequences.

She gripped the edge of the basin as panic surged up her spine. What was she going to do? Leo had made it all too clear that he didn't want to be a father again. He wouldn't bring a baby into the world which didn't have two parents to love it. Except that there *was* a baby. It was growing inside her right that minute. She touched her stomach.

There was a tiny miracle in there.

She went back into her bedroom and sat on the bed. What was she going to do? She wouldn't get rid of it. The baby was a part of her. A part of Leo. She put her hands over her face.

'Oh, how do I tell him?'

Then a sudden coldness prickled her skin. She couldn't tell him. Not ever. If she did, he would do the 'right' thing — he'd offer to marry her. She knew that instinctively. He would not flinch from his duty. And she didn't want to be a duty. Her fingers clutched at the bed clothes, tightening painfully. She didn't want to marry him knowing he didn't love her. She wanted . . . *damn it* . . . she was in love with him!

The revelation flooded over her. She loved Leo. Loved him with a passion and longing that was like a deep fever — one that she'd never recover from. Her father had been right. How ironic that William should realise her emotions before she did.

Amelia groaned. Her palms were

damp with anxiety, and in her heart a mixture of emotions swirled. She was terrified of being pregnant. Gloriously happy at the thought of a tiny baby all of her own. And over all that, her heart soared with her love for Leo.

'You've messed up big this time,' she told herself. She could almost see William shaking his head at the situation she'd created. But she didn't care about what he thought, she reminded herself fiercely. Leo shot into her mind. She did care about his opinion. And that was the problem. If she told him she was expecting their baby, he'd be furious, then insist upon marriage. If she didn't tell him, and he found out . . . She couldn't begin to imagine how angry he'd be with her. She'd have deserted him, just like Grace did.

Slowly Amelia pushed up from the bed on weak legs. What if he never found out? And in that instant, she knew what she had to do. She must leave Grenville and never return, even if it meant tearing her heart out. Even if she never saw Leo and Lucio again. She pressed her knuckles to her mouth to keep from screaming. It was so unfair! But what else was she to do? The only solution meant keeping her baby and losing the only man she'd ever loved. Forever. The question rose like smoke. Was she brave enough to go through with it?

Lucio started to cry. She went quickly through to the nursery and picked him up from his cot. He quietened immediately, his soft face burrowing into her arm. Her eyes dampened. She loved this little boy. What damage was she going to do by leaving him abruptly with no goodbyes? She could only hope he'd forget her quickly. Children were resilient, weren't they?

Leo would hire another nanny for his son, and Lucio would be fine. She tried to ignore the jealous surge that brought. Another woman in the child's life, who would care for him and watch him grow. But what claim did Amelia have on him? *None*. There, that was the harsh truth. She was nothing but Leo's employee. She'd have been gone soon anyway, and was simply leaving a little earlier than planned, that was all. There was a lump in her throat now. She tried to swallow and couldn't. No matter how logical it sounded, the pain wouldn't go.

Over the weeks, she had grown incredibly fond of her charge. He was thriving. The colic had gone, thanks to her hard work and loving care. He was growing fast, his features changing all the time. Growing more like his father every day. She felt a pang in her stomach. She had loved seeing his progress, and was going to miss him dreadfully.

She took her time showering and dressing — using delaying tactics, because she dreaded seeing Leo. Was it possible he would sense the change in her? She shook her head. She could do this; see him once more. It was all she'd have to last a lifetime.

★ ★ ★

'Joe and Neeva have left for America,'
Leo was saying to Mora outside on the
veranda. Amelia heard him from outside the door where she hovered,
plucking up her courage to see him.
She took a deep, fortifying breath and
walked outside to join them.

'Good morning, Amelia.' Mora smiled
to welcome her, then frowned as she
turned back to Leo. 'They must have
got the last flight off the island.'

'Why have the planes stopped flying?'
Amelia asked, and was pleased to hear
she sounded normal. She could barely
look at Leo, afraid her love for him
would shine out; that he'd see it, or that
somehow he'd know she was carrying
his baby. She felt changed, and certain
it must show. She forced a casual smile
and let her gaze fall on Leo's face.
Immediately her chest clenched. He
looked awful. There were deep lines
grooved down the sides of his mouth
and shadows under his eyes.

'There's a tropical storm approaching,' he said, but his golden eyes held hers as if searching for something.

Her breath caught and she couldn't look away. Mora had bustled inside to make breakfast. She and Leo were alone. But there was a gulf between them, invisible and impenetrable. A sadness, so intense it was sweet, hit her. She had to give him up. Deliberately she looked away and forced her shoulders down. *Relax. Pretend nothing is wrong.* Nothing that Leo's keen senses could pick up on. He knew her too well now. If he had an inkling of what she intended . . .

'How can there be a storm?' she asked. 'Look at the day; it's breezy and warm. Actually, it's the nicest day I've seen so far.'

'Believe me, there is a storm. A big one. There are sea swells and the wind is picking up. What you're feeling as a light breeze will be a strong gale by evening. Trinita will be battening down all hatches by tonight. It's good that Joe and Neeva got out.'

'I hope Neeva is feeling better for travelling,' Amelia said. Neeva had suffered very badly from morning sickness. Thinking about pregnancy was like sticking a knife into her skin. She risked a glance at Leo, to find him looking at her.

'Joe told me she's over the worst of it,' Leo said. 'I'm glad for them. They'll make good parents.'

'Because they both want the baby?' What on earth was she doing, stirring a fire-ants' nest with a short stick?

'Yes, of course.'

'There are plenty of one-parent families in the world who manage to bring up a child in a loving environment. Like you and Lucio.'

He nodded. 'That's true. But I imagine any child would rather have both a mother and a father if given the choice. Lucio is no exception.'

But there is no choice for me. Amelia bit her lip.

Leo was tired. No, scratch that — he

was exhausted and hollowed out, unable to sleep and stalking the house at night when everyone else slumbered. He had always loved that time when he had the place to himself. He'd work in his study, getting things done in total peace. But he wasn't at peace anymore. Amelia was never out of his head. He had treated her badly, but he didn't know how to put it right.

He had nothing to offer her. His heart was empty and bruised. He had been truthful with her. *I'm not ready, will never be ready to love again*. He'd been brutally honest and had seen her flinch. But she had to know. It was better to be cruel at the outset, before they got enmeshed in . . . in whatever it was that drew him to her like a magnet.

Now he looked at her afresh. The grey eyes were unreadable, no longer a way for him to understand her. Amelia had finally learned to shade her feelings behind a shutter, because of him. It shouldn't hurt him, but it did. There were delicate traceries of pale blue veins in the hollows under her eyes, and a tiny pulse beat on her temple. Her freckles stood out too darkly on her cheeks.

He wanted to ask her if she was well, but the words failed him. Since the day after the summerhouse he found it impossible to reach her. And he blamed himself. He just didn't know how to fix it. He tried. 'I hope you aren't getting Mora's flu?'

'What makes you say that?' Amelia snapped. She looked unhappy and scared. *Scared?*

'You look . . . ' *You look pale and frightened; and despite that, beautiful and unreachable.* 'You look a little peaky.'

'Peaky? No, I feel perfectly fine, thank you. Don't bother worrying about me. I can look after myself.'

'I know very well you can look after yourself.' He smiled, and there was an answering hint of a curve on her lips. A tiny moment of connection between them. It grew a seed of hope in him, tiny but real.

'So, no need to worry about me. It's all good,' she said brightly. It sounded brittle to his ears.

'Amelia . . . '

'What?'

Amelia, I can't stop thinking about you. About that day in the summerhouse. About making love with you. 'I was going to ask you what you and Lucio are doing today.'

'Oh.' She wrinkled her forehead. She'd been expecting him to say something else. As had he. 'We're going into the town for some shopping. Lucio needs new babygros and other clothes. He's growing so fast.'

'No.' Leo shook his head firmly, 'No town today. It's too risky with the storm on its way.'

She looked stormy herself. So, she still didn't like to be told what to do.

'Please,' he added gently.

She nodded. 'Okay. If you think it's going to be a problem, we can go another day. Maybe we'll do some baking instead.'

'Thank you.'

'Leo . . . ' she called as he made to walk away.

He turned back. She looked small and alone. It was an odd thought. He shook it from him. She was petite, which was part of her charm. But she wasn't alone. She had him and Lucio and Mora for company. So why did that feeling linger?

'Yes?'

'I wanted to thank you, too, for taking a chance on me; for giving me the job when you had so many reasons not to trust me. I hope . . . I hope you feel that trust has been justified.'

Leo frowned. He stepped back towards her. Not too close. He couldn't trust his own reflexes if he smelt her warm skin, her scent of violets, the smell that was singularly and uniquely her.

'I do trust you implicitly. I'm very glad I gave you the post of nanny to my son. You've done a wonderful job of looking after him. You've got rid of his colic and he's a healthy, contented baby. Yes, I'd say you've worked a miracle or two.'

Something shifted in her expression, as if some decision had been reached and a weight shed from her. 'I'm glad,' she said simply.

'You don't have to thank me,' Leo replied, uneasy for no reason he could put a finger on. 'We're doing all right, aren't we? All of us here at Grenville.'

She looked suddenly so sad, he wanted to reach out and pull her in close to him; to soak out whatever bothered her so.

'Yes, we're all doing well,' she said quietly. 'Lucio most of all. He's a credit to you.' Now her eyes rose to meet his.

'Amelia, is there something wrong? Something you want to talk to me about?'

'No, there's no need to talk. We've said everything we need to.'

He wouldn't pretend to misunderstand her. She was referring to their conversation the day after the summerhouse, when he had made it plain how he felt. He reached for her. She stepped back, her eyes suspiciously shiny.

'Please let me go. I have to organise Lucio's day. You know how much energy your son has.' She brushed past him and he let her go.

*   *   *

Leo's sense of unease could not be shaken off. He had avoided the house after a quick breakfast. There was plenty of work to be done before the tropical storm hit the island. He rounded up the men and gave out tasks. Any loose items, big or small, had to be fastened down. Grenville's old shutters had to be closed over the windows of the house. The workers' houses must be secured. There were branches near to the walls that needed to be chopped before they fractured and blew across, causing damage. There was no time to think of Amelia.

But he did anyway. He played over their conversation like an endless loop. It wasn't until he had the machete in his hand, slicing and hacking at a palm tree that leaned dangerously towards the house, that he got it. In an instant the weapon dropped from his hand. He ignored the querulous shouts of his helpers.

He took the distance from the jungle to Grenville House in a fast lope. Up the steps, through the entrance hall, into the kitchen. Baking. Wasn't that what she'd said? He saw Mora and Lucio's surprised faces. The flour and sugar. Ceramic bowls. Wooden spoons. But no Amelia. Even as his heart sank he found no surprise there.

She hadn't been making idle conversation that morning on the veranda. She had been saying goodbye. He made the turn on the stairs and burst into her room. There on the bed was a single sheet of paper, a scribbled note with his name on it. Apart from that, the room was empty.

★ ★ ★

Amelia hurried along the dirt road, barely seeing in front of her for a glazing of unshed tears. Soon she would reach the tarmac surface where the road widened and headed for the town. A taxi would be waiting there for her. She tightened her grip on the pull-along suitcase as its wheels protested over the grit and potholed surface. She had all her worldly possessions inside it; had left nothing at Grenville, no trace of her except the letter to Leo.

Even that was brief. She could hardly tell him about the baby, so it said only that she had to leave, and not to try to find her; that she was sorry and hoped he and Lucio would have a good life.

What more was there to say? That she loved him so intensely it was a torment to leave him. That she promised to bring up their baby in the best way she could. She'd make sure it had enough love from her for both parents. Now the tears came and she wiped them away with her sleeve.

It had been beyond hard to leave Lucio. She had set up the baking activity while he gurgled happily and bounced in his baby chair. He had given her the sweetest smile when she stroked his soft cheek in farewell. Then she had called Mora and asked nicely if she wouldn't mind taking over for a while, as she had a headache, and not to call her; she'd have an hour's rest and be down. Mora, being the kind, considerate woman she was, told her to take as much time as she needed; there was no hurry.

But there was a hurry. Amelia had to leave Grenville before Leo came back to the house from the estate. Once he returned she'd have missed her chance. She had to get away immediately, and had packed quickly. She paused only once, and that was when she came upon her sandals. Leo's gift to her.

Then she'd packed them up too, on top of everything else, zipped and ready.

She had managed to get downstairs and out a side door without Mora or Lucio hearing her. Then it was easy to get outside the walls and call for a taxi, thanking God that her mobile had a reception — just enough to order a car before the line crackled and broke. The coming storm was causing electrical problems already.

She heard the workers crashing about in the jungle, hammering and sawing, shouting commands. She prayed that Leo wouldn't appear at the jungle edge and see her. Fleeing like an intruder, she soon disappeared along the track and out of sight of the big house.

Now, with an overwhelming sense of relief, she saw the taxi waiting for her. Amelia caught a sob, rubbed her face dry and tried to look calm. She had made it. The taxi driver lifted up her suitcase into the car boot.

She looked back once. There was nothing but greenery. But behind it and along a bend was Grenville House and the estate — gone, out of her sight forever, and taking with it everything she cared about in the world: the man she loved; his little boy; a whole way of life she'd once crazily imagined she could have.

The taxi dropped her off at the small harbour. She shivered; the wind had got up, no longer a light and playful breeze. The gusts meant business. There was a howling to the gale as it blasted in from the sea and lifted her hair from her face. The sea was dark grey, and it rose and fell in huge waves that were bigger than she'd ever seen.

Amelia fumbled in her suitcase for a cardigan. She had brought one. Not that she'd needed it with the humid heat. But now . . . yes, it was actually cold. She twisted her mouth at the irony. She was now so accustomed to the island heat that she felt freezing. How would she cope with the English weather?

She stilled. She hadn't thought this

through at all. She had wanted to be gone from Grenville. But to where? Not to England. Not back to London. *Think! Think!* She hugged her arms round her body, urging her brain to function. The cardigan helped thaw her a little. Where would she go?

'First things first, get off the island,' she muttered. 'Once I'm on the mainland, I can decide where I'm going.'

She pulled all her reserves of courage and determination together. *I can do this. I am stronger now than when I arrived on Trinita. Leo has made me strong.* Plus, she didn't only have herself to protect now. She had her baby. Their baby.

Shoulders back and head up proudly, Amelia dragged her suitcase down the cobbled steps of the harbour towards the fishing boats. They bobbed crazily on the swollen sea water. She approached one of the grizzled skippers. Most of the fishermen were in a group, smoking cigarettes and arguing in the local language; she could make out only that they were angry and that the sea was to blame.

'Excuse me,' she shouted over the sighing of the wind. 'I need to get off the island. Is there a ferry, or can I get a boat here?'

The old man shouted back to her but at first she didn't understand what he was saying. He had a thick island accent and mingled his English with patois.

'Sorry, I didn't catch what you said?'

'No boats, no boats.' He waved his hands at her as if she were crazy. 'No one leaving the island today. Big storm!'

Her stomach seemed to contract at his words as she finally understood. She was completely stranded. There were no flights from Trinita airport, and no boats prepared to battle the storm to the mainland.

She could not go back to Grenville. She stood hesitantly, a slight figure buffeted by the increasing ferocity of the weather. She had never felt more alone in her whole life.

14

The storm had raged for two whole days, and the island had been battered and bruised by its passing. Boats were lifted from the sea and dumped far inland. Roofs were ripped from houses and smashed to the ground. Cars and trees had been overturned. Luckily no one was killed, but there were injuries.

Leo swore silently as he surveyed his own roof. There were many tiles missing. The house of one of the workers had the trunk of a tree embedded in it. There were brush and palm fronds all over the courtyard. Still, they had been lucky; nobody on the estate had been hit by flying debris.

Where was she? Wherever Amelia had vanished to, he prayed she was safe. He alternated between worry and anger: worry that she had been hurt by the savagery of the storm, and anger that she'd left him without a word; that she hadn't trusted him enough to tell him why she felt she had to go right then and there. She hadn't waited to finish her contract after all. What had happened to make her go so abruptly?

He dragged a ladder from one of the outhouses across to the main wall of the house and slammed it so hard against the surface that some of the roughcast broke away and fell. *Damn it*. He couldn't concentrate. The heat seared his forehead. The weather after the storm was hot and calm. He was thirsty.

He walked over and into the house, intending to get a drink. Lucio was screaming at the top of his lungs and drumming his legs as he rolled on the floor on a blue blanket. Mora looked worn out. Leo swooped him up testily. Lucio's mouth opened in a circle of shock.

'Stop that. Do you hear me? Stop it now. I can't stand it,' he boomed.

Lucio stared at him uncertainly, then

burst into tears. Leo gave an exasperated sigh and pushed him into Mora's arms, taking the glass in exchange. 'Do something,' he commanded in desperation.

Mora shook her head, her expression carefully neutral while Lucio was with her. She cuddled the small boy upstairs with soft words and Leo was left in the entrance hall, his head buzzing with noise. Could she have reached the mainland? Or worse, had she tried to make the journey across the narrows and . . . He couldn't finish his train of thought. There had been no word of a capsized boat on the local news channel. He'd have heard for sure if that had happened. No, he had to believe she was still on Trinita. He paced backwards and forwards, his brow furrowed. How was it possible? Where had she gone?

Mora came back downstairs alone. She stood on the bottom step, arms folded across her chest, and looked at him.

'What?'

'You know what, Leo. Don't try to pretend otherwise. You've upset your son. He's never heard you shout at him so angrily.'

'He needs to learn. He has to have self-discipline for when he's older. When he goes to school.'

'Self-discipline? Like his father? I see no discipline here. I see a man like the proverbial bear with the sore head.'

Leo wanted to growl like a bear. Unfortunately he'd known Mora Sorrento for far too long. She was the housekeeper, but she was so much more. She was an old and trusted friend; one of the few who could tell him the unpainted truth.

'It's been a rough couple of days,' he began.

'Yes, for all of us,' Mora agreed gently. 'But for you most of all. Don't bother to argue with me. I know you're missing her. We all are. Lucio wants her home and so do I.'

'If she wanted to be here, then she

wouldn't have left,' Leo said forcefully. 'She clearly doesn't want to work here anymore.'

'You know there must be more to it than that. She left so suddenly. Perhaps she was upset?' Mora shrugged helplessly. 'I wish I knew what made her go.'

'We don't need her,' Leo said. 'It's finished. We move on. I'll hire another nanny for my son. She isn't the only English nanny in the world.'

Mora looked at him with pity. 'Leo, you're angry and impatient, and the workers are unhappy. They tell me so. It's very unlike the boss, they say. But they don't like it. They want the old master of Grenville back. So for all our sakes, please, please go and get her. Bring her home.'

When he didn't budge, she sighed and spoke again. 'Do I have to spell it out? You're obviously in love with her. So sort it out. Make it right.'

It struck him hard, like a blow to the midriff. Mora was right. All his pining, his fear and his fury at Amelia Knight was because he was in love with her. His heart had opened up for her whether he'd wanted it to or not. All his defences had broken down without him noticing. Now with her absence, he was opened up to new pain that made him as vulnerable as a kitten. *There's a level of emotion, an intensity of it, that I cannot ever feel.* That was what he'd told Amelia when he'd described why they couldn't, shouldn't get involved. But he felt the intensity now. The level of his emotion was topping the sky. He needed her. He had to find her, to tell her. But where was she?

He groaned and ran his fingers through his hair in frustration. 'She's gone, and I don't know how to find her.'

Mora smiled. 'Yes you do, if you think for a moment. Where is the only place she'd go?'

A pause. Outside a parrot squawked and a monkey shrieked. Familiar sounds. She'd go somewhere safe — a place she was familiar with, where she'd get a warm welcome.

Leo snapped his fingers. Within moments he had the vehicle keys in the ignition, and the jeep bounded out of the gates and onto the dirt road.

★ ★ ★

'Now, he makes it home. He takes his time about it, my son does.' Sancia stood, hands on hips, at her front door. Her black eyes were stern.

'Let me speak to her,' Leo asked wearily.

'Do you deserve to? You've made Amelia very unhappy.'

'She said that?'

'Not in so many words, but I'm not blind. I can see what's going on.'

'There's nothing going on.'

'Yes, that's the problem. You're too slow. You let her slip away from you.'

'Mama — ' he warned.

She raised her palms up. 'Okay, you can see her. But be nice; she's not well.'

'Amelia's sick? How ill is she? Is it

bad?' His voice rose in panic.

Sancia smiled and took pity on him. 'She'll tell you herself.'

★ ★ ★

She was in the garden, alone. Leo wanted to run and sweep her up in his arms and kiss her. But he held back. Her expression was guarded.

'Hello, Leo. You found me.'

'You didn't make it easy. There was little on your note.' His anger flickered back into a flame.

'I'm sorry, but it seemed for the best.'

'Really? To walk out on us with no explanation, into the storm, was for the best?' He let the sarcasm bite his words and saw her lids squeeze shut before she turned her grey gaze on him fully. He was shocked by the pain he saw there. What was it? What was she hiding? Sancia's words came back to him.

'Are you ill?' he asked. 'Is that why you left?' It made no sense to him.

She flushed and seemed nervous all of a sudden. He had a desire to shake the whole truth out of her. But he trusted her; he'd won that long and hard battle with himself to do so. He trusted her to tell him what she needed to say.

'I'm truly sorry that I left the way I did,' Amelia said, 'but I couldn't see a way out.'

'A way out?' Now Leo was thoroughly confused.

'The problem I was battling was so enormous that there was no other path.'

'And you didn't trust me enough to share it with me?' That hurt more than her leaving. His trust in her wasn't returned.

'I trust you in most things.' Amelia hesitated. 'But in this one thing, I couldn't be sure . . . *can't* be sure that you won't hate me.'

'I could never hate you,' Leo said. His heart was in his mouth. *I could never hate you, because I love you.* So why wouldn't the words come? Because in that moment he was terrified. What if she had no feelings for him?

'Tell me,' he commanded. 'Whatever it is, we can handle it together.'

'I'm pregnant.'

Her words stunned him into silence.

Of course it was a mistake to tell him. Amelia had realised it the moment she opened her mouth. Why, oh why did Leo have to come looking for her? She'd told him quite specifically not to in her note. Not that he was the kind of man to tamely do what he was told. The master of Grenville always made his own mind up, forged his own path. They would always clash. It was inevitable. He wanted to be in charge, but she wanted to make her own decisions too. It would never have worked between them.

His silence was worth a million words, and none of them good. She saw a play of emotions run across his face, and had no idea what he was thinking — until he suddenly pulled her to him and planted a kiss on her mouth.

Surprised, she pushed his chest hard. He backed off one step only.

'What was that for?' she demanded.

'Because I've wanted to kiss you again for days and days. Let me.'

She wanted him to, badly. To feel the tingling sensation of his hard lips and seeking tongue; to revel in his touch. But it wasn't right. He had to leave. He'd want to leave. Hadn't he heard what she'd said about the baby?

'Leo, I said I'm having a baby. Your baby. Aren't you angry with me?'

He looked at her hungrily. She licked her lips nervously and saw his gaze darken. If only he didn't do things to her body. She had to concentrate. And so did he.

'I'm not angry with you, Amelia Knight. I'm past angry.'

'What does that mean?' she asked warily.

He reached for her again and she let him. 'It means that I'm in love with you, and I wish I'd told you, so that you wouldn't have run away from me.'

Now it was Amelia's turn for stunned silence while her brain caught up. Leo loved her? 'But you told me . . .'

'I was a fool,' he interrupted her. 'I believed my heart to be so broken by Grace that I was incapable of ever falling in love again. But when I lost you . . . I've been through hell trying to think where you'd gone.'

'I was trying to leave the island,' she admitted, 'but there was no transport off it. I was desperate, and the only place I could think of was your parents' home. Sancia and Jose have been wonderful to me. I made them promise not to tell you where I was. Your mother begged, but she kept her word. How did you find me?'

'I realised you couldn't leave Trinita during the storm. I wracked my brain and came up with nothing, until Mora guessed it. Where else could you have gone? This is home.'

'You're in love with me?' Amelia said, wanting to check. Wanting to hear him say it.

He showed her instead. When she managed a breath between kisses, he whispered it in her ear.

'I love you too,' she whispered back.

His body answered hers, and for a long moment they stayed wrapped in each other until Amelia pulled away. 'I didn't tell your mother about the baby. She guessed.'

Leo rolled his eyes. 'You can't keep a secret safely from my mama. She'll be overjoyed to think of another Grenville grandchild.'

'And you? Are you overjoyed?' Amelia asked quietly.

'I'm happy it's only a baby.'

'I don't understand. It's not *only* a baby. This is a huge responsibility, and one I'm not asking you to share if you don't want to.'

He grinned. 'My mother said you were ill. I was terrified you had something seriously wrong with your health. So after that, a baby is good news. And, darling,' he added with a tender kiss to the side of her mouth, 'it's a responsibility I definitely want to share with you.'

'But you were so against the idea of having a child. You asked me if it was safe the day we . . . we made love.'

He grimaced. 'I'm sorry; I didn't handle the situation well that day. I was blown away by my feelings for you. I think I had already fallen in love with you but just couldn't admit it to myself. I argued that Grace had spoiled me for anyone else; and yes, I said a baby would be a disaster. But when I found out the day before that Joe and Neeva were expecting their first, I was deeply jealous. I imagined what our baby would look like.'

She snuggled into him and glanced up. 'What do you think he'd look like?'

'I think *she* will be a miniature Amelia, with beautiful golden curls and big gorgeous eyes. What about you?'

'I think *he* will be just like his daddy, with unruly black hair and eyes the colour of forest honey.'

'We'll get married as soon as

possible. At Grenville,' Leo said decisively.

'Do I get a say in this?' Amelia said, somewhat irked. There it was once more — the clash of two people who both liked to be in charge. Maybe she was right, and it wouldn't work.

He raised an eyebrow in surprise. 'I thought you loved Grenville?'

'I do, of course I do,' she said. 'But I don't want you organising the whole thing without asking me what I want.'

'I'm not doing that. I'm suggesting a scenario that we'd both enjoy.'

'Without asking me what I want,' she persisted.

'What *do* you want, apart from biting my head off?'

'This isn't going to work,' she said, shaking her head. 'I don't like being told what to do, and you like giving the orders. You need a different kind of wife.'

'It *is* going to work,' Leo said firmly, 'because we'll *make* it work. I don't want a little mouse of a wife; I want a woman who knows her own mind. A woman who's prepared to move half a world away to find her place of happiness. A strong, courageous sort of woman.'

She smiled slowly. 'There's something else, Leo.'

'Hmm?'

'You haven't actually asked me to marry you. You've told me where I'm getting married and when. But nothing else.' She shrugged.

His mouth quirked. She glared at him. With a muffled word that she didn't care to identify, Leo got down on one knee. She saw Sancia and Jose watching out of the large window under the bougainvillea and hid a smile.

'Amelia Knight, will you marry me?'

She grinned outright now. 'Yes, please. You can get up now.' She kissed him to seal their agreement, and Leo kissed her back with equal passion.

'So, my darling, where would you like to get married, and when in the seasons would suit you best?' Leo asked innocently.

She pretended to consider it, pressing one finger to her chin and tilting her head. 'I think I'd like to get married as soon as possible. At the Grenville Estate. What do you think?'

'That's an admirable suggestion, my love. Your wish is my command.'

They would always argue, she guessed. But making up was bound to be interesting.

Sancia and Jose came hurrying out of the house with a bottle of champagne. 'We must celebrate,' Sancia said, hugging them both. 'My favourite son is getting married. It's wonderful news!'

'How did you know I'd proposed?' Leo asked, not sounding in the least surprised.

'Of course we were watching you from the window,' his mother said. 'You're slow, but you get there in the end, Leo. That's what matters.'

She turned to Jose to tell him how to open the bottle of sparkling fizz and Amelia risked a whispered comment: 'You're her favourite son?'

'She says that to all of us, depending on how well we've pleased her,' Leo murmured back quietly, so the older couple wouldn't hear.

'Will Lucio be happy with a new mother and a baby brother or sister?' Amelia asked uncertainly, thinking of his transition from only child to one of two at the very least.

'Lucio loves you already,' Leo said, 'and he's young enough to make that change easily. It's a safe bet that he'll be happy with both of us as his parents. Once we've shared a celebratory drink with my parents, we'll go and see him. If you agree?' he added.

'I couldn't agree more.' Amelia sighed with perfect contentedness.

A warm island breeze teased her hair and cooled her skin kindly. It brought with it the fragrance of the blossoms in the garden and the voices of her new family around her. Her husband-to-be stood proudly with his arm around her, and her ready-made son was waiting at home for them. Amelia put a protective hand on her stomach. Leo's large hand covered hers. He kissed her with such tenderness, and she knew she had found a forever kind of love.

Epilogue

'Ouch! Lucio just grabbed my hair!' Lara howled.

'Come along, young man. Leave your cousin alone,' Leo said, picking his son up and tousling his niece's hair in sympathy.

Lucio struggled to be put down. A tantrum threatened.

'Be nice, now. It's Catherine's first birthday,' Amelia said, laughing.

They were in the midst of a Grenville family party — the best kind of party, in Amelia's opinion. She'd morphed happily from being pretty much without any kind of family to being part of Leo's large, noisy extended family. It was their daughter Catherine's first birthday today and they were all there to celebrate with her.

She looked over at Leo, now holding his little girl. She had his dark hair, but curlier, and Amelia's grey eyes. They had named her for Amelia's mother, and she wished her mum was alive to see her namesake. Leo winked at her and she saw his sexy dimple appear as he grinned. Her nerves tingled. He still had the power to arouse her; the attraction they felt for each other never failed, instead growing with every day.

'Mummy,' Lucio said, running to her and burrowing his dark head in her middle. He'd started calling her Mummy as soon as he could speak, which she and Leo were both very happy about. There had been no problems at all. Grace had never got in touch to ask about her son; but Amelia knew that if she did, they would all manage the situation somehow. If Grace wanted to get to know Lucio, Amelia and Leo would help to make that happen. But for now they were busy with their little family, and all the commotion a toddler and baby could bring.

Amelia stroked Lucio's hair and

kissed him. 'What is it, *bebe*? Do you want some cake?'

He hugged her hard. 'Cake.'

'At least she's walking now,' Leo said, placing his daughter down on her two sturdy legs. 'Why don't you take your sister over to Lara and Kenny? Look, they're showing Sara how to build a tower with the plastic bricks.'

With a show of reluctance, Lucio took Catherine's sticky hand and led her slowly across the patio to their big cousins. But Amelia saw the care he took with her. They were okay together, as long as Lucio had it all his own way. She wondered how long that would last as Catherine's personality developed.

'What's on your mind?' Leo kissed her swiftly and put his arm around her shoulders.

'Just wondering if we should consider a brother for our two. What do you think?'

'You know I want a big family. Besides . . . ' His fingers trailed along her arm, prickling her nerves sweetly.

'It'll be fun practising.'

'Agreed.' She twined her fingers with his and felt their strength and warmth. She stroked the palm of his hand with her thumb and felt him take a sudden breath. A promise for later. Then the moment was broken as the others came out of the house bearing food and drinks.

'Where were you two? I had to rely on Joe and Daniel, and they ate more than they carried,' Sancia grumbled, pretending to be annoyed. Joe and Neeva were over visiting from the States, and had brought their daughter Sara with them.

'I'll go and give Wendy a hand,' Amelia said. Wendy had made the birthday cake and was putting the finishing touches to the icing on the top.

'No, no, she's fine,' Sancia warned. 'The artist is at work. Better to wait until she's ready for you. Where's Neeva?'

'Mopping Sara up,' Joe said with a

grin. 'She's managed to dump a whole bottle of chocolate sauce over her front. More fun than building bricks, I guess.'

His tone suggested fatherly pride in his daughter. Sara had been born a month before Catherine, the two girls bringing Sancia and Jose's number of grandchildren to five — which was sufficient, Leo had teased his mother. Sancia's response was that there was plenty room for more, especially at the large Grenville estate, which was crying out for children to fill its sprawling space.

The table was set with a spread of food and drink, and the day was warm and dry with a light, gentle breeze. The family settled round it and began to pass out plates and cutlery. The kids ran to join the party, jostling for biscuits and sweets.

'Have you heard from your father?' Sancia asked Amelia.

She shook her head. 'I don't expect to.'

She tried hard not to be bitter. At

Leo's insistence they had sent William Knight an invitation to their wedding. She hadn't wanted to, as she was still angry at him. But Leo had thought it would be closure for her. Besides, it was the right thing to do. She'd allowed him to send it. There had been a sneaking hope he might turn up, even give her away as father of the bride. But there had been no response. Not even a letter or card to say he would not come. Nothing.

When Catherine was born, they had sent a letter with a photograph of her. Again he had not replied. Amelia had made a decision then never to contact him again. If he couldn't be bothered to come to her wedding or acknowledge his only grandchild, then she couldn't be bothered trying to keep in touch with him either. There was a saying she'd heard somewhere, that rotten fathers could make surprisingly better grandfathers. If that was the case generally, it certainly wasn't true of her own situation.

'You must try again,' Sancia insisted. 'It's family. Nothing is more important.' She spread her hands to encompass her husband and sons, daughters-in-law and grandchildren.

'Mama,' Leo warned. He knew what hell Amelia had been through with this.

'Okay, I'm just saying.' His mother flashed her dark eyes meaningfully.

'William doesn't want to know,' Amelia said with a small smile. 'He doesn't care about me or Catherine. He had his chance and now it's gone. I'd rather we didn't mention my father at all.'

'If that's what you want.' Leo's mother inclined her head, but Amelia knew she didn't agree. For the Grenvilles, family came first. Anything else was unthinkable.

There was a huge pile of gifts for the birthday girl. After they had eaten, Leo and Amelia set Catherine down on a cushion and helped her unwrap her presents. Soon she was surrounded by a mound of soft toys and teddies. There was one gift left. It was oblong and wrapped exquisitely in shiny blue paper.

'Who is this from?' Amelia asked. 'You've all given her such lovely toys.'

'One way to find out.' Leo passed it to her. 'Open it up. Catherine's too busy with her new ragdoll.'

'It came in the post here; Mora redirected it from Grenville,' Sancia said. 'I took off the parcel paper and that was inside. No card or label.'

'What was the posting address?' Amelia asked.

'Sorry, I didn't take note. Should I have?'

'It doesn't matter.' Because she was pretty sure she knew who'd sent it. Finally.

She ripped off the paper to find a hand mirror. It was beautiful, looked expensive and was totally unsuitable for a one-year-old. She guessed William had sent his personal assistant to buy the gift. There was a tag attached by a silk string to the mirror's handle. It simply said, 'For Catherine'.

'Excuse me,' Amelia said. She escaped into the cool interior of the house, not sure what to feel or think. Leo followed her in and cradled her in his arms. She felt the pressure of his lips on the top of her head; felt his love for her in the strength of his embrace. His need to protect her and shield her from hurt. And she loved him for it; loved him with all her fierce might. She didn't need her father. She had all she wanted right here.

'It's a start,' she heard Leo say.

She pulled back a little and stared up at him. 'What?'

'It might be all that he's capable of. Your father. But he sent the mirror, and that's a start.'

'He probably didn't send it,' Amelia said drily. 'His assistant bought it, wrapped it and sent it.'

'What about the writing on the tag?'

She thought a moment. It was her father's handwriting. Maybe Leo was right. And maybe she could start to come to terms with it. He was never going to be the father she had so desperately wanted as a child, but perhaps she could accept what he was able to give.

She nodded. Then she took her husband's loving hand and let him lead her outside to join her family in the warm Trinita sunshine. Where she belonged.